MAKE STORY TIME A SPECIAL TIME FOR YOU AND YOUR CHILD

"Hansel and Gretel"

Grimm's fairy tales often feature a wicked stepmother—but you don't have to! By telling stories yourself you can change the villainess, eliminate gender stereotyping, and convey the message *you* want ... or even change an ending to one more appropriate for your child.

"Chicken Licken"

In this story of a chicken with a vivid imagination that runs afoul, you get to repeat the delightful names of Foxy Woxy, Goosey Loosey, and the other animals who join Chicken Licken to tell the king the sky is falling. To discuss the story, ask your child, "Do you think the sky is falling when an acorn falls?" and talk about when to believe what another person tells you.

"The Boy Who Cried Wolf"

Aesop's fables end with a moral, and this story lets you show your child that if you lie, nobody will believe you when you tell the truth—and you can ham it up crying "Wolf, Wolf!" for lots of giggles from your audience.

Tell Me a Fairy Tale
The start of a new family tradition

BILL ADLER, JR., is the president of Adler & Robin Books, Inc., a literary agency and book packaging company. He is the author of more than a dozen books, but it is his role as the father of two little girls that makes him qualified to write *this* book.

Tell Me a Fairy Tale

A Parent's Guide to Telling Magical and Mythical Stories

BILL ADLER, JR.

A PLUME BOOK

PLUME
Published by the Penguin Group
Penguin Books USA Inc., 375 Hudson Street,
New York, New York 10014, U.S.A.
Penguin Books Ltd, 27 Wrights Lane, London W8 5TZ, England
Penguin Books Australia Ltd, Ringwood, Victoria, Australia
Penguin Books Canada Ltd, 10 Alcorn Avenue,
Toronto, Ontario, Canada M4V 3B2
Penguin Books (N.Z.) Ltd, 182–190 Wairau Road,
Auckland 10, New Zealand

Penguin Books Ltd, Registered Offices:
Harmondsworth, Middlesex, England

First published by Plume, an imprint of Dutton Signet,
a division of Penguin Books USA Inc.

First Printing, April, 1995
10 9 8 7 6 5 4 3 2 1

Ⓟ REGISTERED TRADEMARK—MARCA REGISTRADA

LIBRARY OF CONGRESS CATALOGING-IN-PUBLICATION DATA:
Adler, Bill.
    Tell me a fairy tale : a parent's guide to telling magical and mythical stories /
Bill Adler, Jr.
        p.   cm.
    ISBN 0-452-27174-6
    1. Children's literature—Technique.   2. Fairy tales.   I. Title.
PN147.5.A34   1995
398.2—dc20   94-29891
                                                                               CIP

Printed in the United States of America
Set in Century Expanded
Designed by Eve L. Kirch

BOOKS ARE AVAILABLE AT QUANTITY DISCOUNTS WHEN USED TO PROMOTE PRODUCTS
OR SERVICES. FOR INFORMATION PLEASE WRITE TO PREMIUM MARKETING DIVISION,
PENGUIN BOOKS USA INC., 375 HUDSON STREET, NEW YORK, NEW YORK 10014.

To baby Claire

Acknowledgments

My greatest thanks go to the wonderful creators of these fairy tales. Next, I want to thank my agent, Jane Dystel. Also lending a great helping hand were Peggy Robin, the mother of my two story listeners. Beth Pratt-Dewey, Karin McDonald, and Renee Marchese contributed much time, thought, and assistance to the retelling of these stories. Thanks, too, to Deb Brody, ace senior editor at Plume.

Contents

Introduction

Fairy tales are great fun. They impart wisdom, morals, history.

But even if fairy tales did nothing to improve the minds and souls of the little people we love so much, they would still be fun to tell—and listen to.

Children love fairy tales; they can listen to them hour after hour—and sometimes do. They love the magic, the colorful costumes, the talking animals. They love giants and tiny people. They love the rhythm of fairy tales and they love the story lines.

They love to hear their parents tell magical, mythical tales.

But the problem for many parents is: which fairy tale? We may remember bits of the adventures of Goldilocks, Rumpelstiltskin, Rapunzel, but that's about all. And even if we know the basic outline of a story we may not remember how it ends!

Tell Me a Fairy Tale offers quick—and complete—synopses of the most enjoyable fairy tales. You can think of this book as Cliff's Notes for fairy tales. *Tell Me a Fairy Tale* includes the classics, but it also includes some of the best African-American, Asian, Native American, and European fairy tales.

I conceived this book soon after I got very, very tired of

telling "Goldilocks and the Three Bears" to my then two-and-a-half-year-old daughter, Karen, every single night and nap time. ("Goldilocks" was the only fairy tale I knew well enough to tell.) While there was no real evidence that Karen was tiring of the tale, I was. And when, in the interest of sanity, I skipped a part, like the business about sitting in the chairs, Karen was quick to insist, "The chairs!"

If only I knew something else to tell!

I didn't want to acquire a large collection of fairy tale anthologies. First, a complete collection would be expensive. Second, to actually read the tales aloud from a book would take half an hour each evening. Karen would never let me leave a tale unfinished for the next night. Finally, it's much more enjoyable to *tell* a story than to read one—especially if you know the ending. When you tell a story, there's unlimited flexibility; your imagination can give the tale whatever shape you want. Once you know the basic plot of a story you can embellish it, even personalize it to incorporate your child if you wish. Or you can shorten the story to hasten the advent of dream-time.

So I decided to outline and summarize a year's worth of fairy tales.

Tell Me a Fairy Tale isn't just for telling tales to kids. It's an indispensable reference book for adults who want to remember their childhood. It's a book that takes adults back through time; that lets us remember the words and images of our childhood.

One of the first things you discover when you read or tell fairy tales to your child is that many are frightening—or so they seem to us.

Take the story of Hansel and Gretel, for example. In this tale, two children are captured by a witch who tries to eat them. Pretty frightening stuff. Ultimately, the children prevail and kill the witch in a painful, awful way. But Hansel and Gretel are saved, so the story has a happy ending, as with most fairy tales.

Yet children don't seem scared by these tales, or if they do, they don't reveal their fear. (Psychologists explain this behavior in a number of ways, none of which are terribly relevant to the telling of fairy tales.)*

When you tell a story using *Tell Me A Fairy Tale*, you can make it as frightening or as benign as you want. Let's look at "Hansel and Gretel" again. In the G-rated version, the witch doesn't want to eat the children; she's just trying to frighten them by making scary witch-noises.

See what you can do if you don't stick to the prescribed plot? Another option is to turn out-of-date fairy tales into less sexist or less stereotyped stories, if you prefer. For example, instead of just passively waiting to be rescued by the handsome prince, the fair maiden can be plotting and attempting her escape.

One twist I like to make in "Goldilocks" comes at the end, when Goldilocks is discovered sleeping in the baby bear's bed. Goldilocks is still very tired, so she runs all the way home to her crib to take a nap. My daughter, Karen, insists on completing "Goldilocks" with the "nap" even if I forget—and then puts her head down on the pillow.

The stories in *Tell Me a Fairy Tale* lack some of the details that appear in the full-blown versions. So feel free to add as many details as you want. Describe clothes, shoes, hats, houses, rooms, sounds, what the characters look like, gardens, individual trees, pictures on the walls, food on the table, window coverings, smells, the sky that day—anything you want. Is the house big, the air cool, the leaves green or turning colors, the fireplace lit? How do the characters walk, smile, sound? Is the house made of wood or stone, and is it covered with ivy? You get the idea. Add dialogue, too. Make up the

---

*But since I mentioned it, here's one theory: Children have a fear that their parents will die and leave them. Telling children about scary things, and then showing them that there are happy endings, soothes their anxieties.

words—after all, the original storytellers did. Feel free, of course, to incorporate elements of your child into the tale— your daughter's name or your son's clothes, for example.

Most of all, keep an eye on your child. Vary the rhythm of the story as appropriate. If your child is falling asleep, by all means, continue talking about the colors, shapes, and smells of the objects in the story—such details help summon dream-time. If your son or daughter loves animals (what child doesn't?), then add more critters to your version than there were in the original. If your child isn't excited about cleaning his or her room, maybe some of the characters in your stories should clean up a lot.

For the sake of consistency, and to please my eighth-grade English teacher, all these stories have been told in the past tense. But some tales are best told in the present tense; others in the past. Use the tense that seems best to you.

You'll note that each story begins with a very brief summary, meant to provide the basic framework for the story's plot. Then there are character sketches to provide the raw material for creating the individuals who inhabit these tales. They are listed so that you won't forget anybody. Then the story is actually told. Finally, there are suggestions on how you might tell the story, and how you could modify it.

In *Tell Me a Fairy Tale* you'll find a wide variety of fairy tales, including the classic Mother Goose and Grimm brothers stories. There are also some Bible tales, and some stories from other cultures. These less well known stories are a good way of broadening your child's knowledge of the world.

Fairy tales contain many gruesome elements: murder, boiling children alive—things that would earn a modern movie an R rating. For the sake of accuracy, I've left these stories as close to the originals as possible, retaining the blood and gore. But that doesn't mean you have to tell all the "scary parts" to your children. Plots can be, and in many cases should be, changed. In the "How to Tell This Story" sections I suggest how.

Many fairy tales and fables don't make a whole lot of sense to adults. The plots don't hold together, the characters' motivations aren't credible. So what? The stories *do* make sense to children.

In many of the original stories, characters do not have names. So create your own.

Magic is the principal ingredient in all fairy tales. Don't skimp here. Children have no trouble believing, and the more magic, the more fun.

You are the storyteller, which makes you a central character in each story. Change the pitch of your voice to talk like a woman, like a man, like a child, even like an animal. Vary the rhythm of your words. Be out of breath when it's called for; speak quietly or loudly as the role requires. Sound effects—whistling, stomping your foot, clapping, gasping, snapping a finger—may be part of the story, too.

Finally, remember that every fairy tale begins, "Once upon a time . . ."

Tell Me a Fairy Tale was completed just in the nick of time. Karen, who is now nearly three and a half and has never tired of stories, has a baby sister, Claire, who's nine months. Soon it's going to be Claire's turn to explore the wonderful world of fairy tales.

Aladdin

Summary

In Persia a wicked sorcerer tricked Aladdin into finding a magic lamp with a genie in it; he also gave him a magic ring that had its own accompanying genie. Aladdin quickly discovered how to use the magic ring and lamp to create a life of comfort for his mother and himself. He fell in love with and married a princess after plying her father, the sultan, with many valuable gifts. In time, the wicked sorcerer returned to Persia to claim the lamp and tricked the princess into giving it to him. He then stole her away to Africa. Aladdin followed them and, with his wife, devised a scheme to kill the sorcerer. He and the princess returned to Persia, but then the sorcerer's brother came to avenge his death. Aladdin dispatched this evil sorcerer as well. He and the princess lived a long and peaceful life, and Aladdin ruled the kingdom after the sultan died.

The Characters

Aladdin: An idle boy with no aspiration. His father was dead and he lived with his mother. The sorcerer thought he was dull, but he was just not motivated. Aladdin was very good-natured and had a sense of fair play.

Aladdin's mother: She loved her boy and helped him win over the princess. She loved her daughter-in-law, and she lived in the palace with the couple.

The princess: Beautiful. Bad judge of character—sometimes.

The sultan: He was greedy and gave his daughter to the man who could give the most spectacular gifts, which of course Aladdin could.

The evil sorcerer: He knew about a powerful genie in a magic lamp, but he could get the lamp only if someone of pure heart gave it to him. He thought Aladdin was dim enough to do it.

The evil sorcerer's brother: Angry and out for revenge.

The ring genie: Used only in emergencies.

The lamp genie: He could bestow the most fabulous gifts imaginable, and his power seemingly had no end. But there were some things even he wouldn't do.

The Plot

Aladdin was an idle boy who spent his days playing with other children in the streets. He wouldn't learn his father's tailoring trade, and so when his father died, Aladdin had no profession—except play, which suited him exactly.

An evil sorcerer had use for such a boy. He approached Aladdin in the streets and introduced himself as his father's long-lost brother. After supping with Aladdin and his mother, he proposed to help Aladdin get started in business. Everyone thought this sounded fine. So he bought the boy some clothes, showed him the city, and the next day took him on a trip, which took them nearly to the mountains. Aladdin was tired, but the sorcerer led him farther and farther until they came to a valley, where the magician bade Aladdin to gather firewood while he made a fire. When the fire was lit, the sorcerer threw a powder on the flames and said a magic charm. The earth trembled and opened in front of them, and a stone door with a brass ring was exposed. Of course, the boy was frightened and tried to flee, but the sorcerer grabbed him and hit him.

Now the magician knew that behind the door lay an enchanted garden containing a magical lamp, a lamp he could have only if someone of pure heart gave it to him. He thought Aladdin would be stupid enough to get the lamp for him, and after that he planned to kill the boy. He told Aladdin where he could find the lamp and promised to share the treasure with him. Then he gave him a magic ring from his own finger. And so Aladdin lifted the stone door and descended underground.

He went through some grand halls into an enchanted garden where he picked some fruit before he found the lamp on the terrace. He returned to the cave's mouth, and the magician told him to toss the lamp out before he came out himself. Aladdin refused, so the sorcerer cast a spell to close up the cave again.

For two days Aladdin stayed in the dark, crying and feeling sorry for himself. Finally he put his hands together to pray and accidentally rubbed the magic ring. A genie appeared and said, "What will you have me do? I am a slave of the ring and will do what you say." Aladdin asked to be released from the cave. He walked home and told his mother his adventures. He showed her the fruits he had gathered in the garden, and they had turned to precious stones.

Naturally Aladdin was famished after his adventures, but his mother had no food in the house. He decided to sell the lamp so they could buy food, and he was polishing it when the genie of the lamp appeared. Aladdin asked for food, so the genie brought food in a silver bowl and on twelve silver plates and wine in two silver cups. Aladdin and his mother ate the food and over time sold the silver to buy more food. When they ran out of food, they asked the genie for more silver dishes, which they sold to buy food. They lived this way for years.

Then one day the sultan commanded all subjects to stay inside with the shutters drawn while his daughter, the princess, went to and from the baths. Aladdin couldn't resist peeking and hid behind the bath door to see her face, which was so beautiful he fell in love immediately. Love so drastically changed his character that at first Aladdin's mother was frightened, but when she learned he intended to marry the princess, she laughed. Still, Aladdin persuaded her to carry his request to the sultan, and she took the precious stones from the enchanted garden to help persuade him.

Aladdin's mother stood in the same place in the palace's audience chamber every day for a week, and finally the sultan asked his vizier to find out what she wanted. She told him and presented the jewels, but the vizier wanted the princess for his own son and persuaded the sultan to wait three months. In that time, he thought, his own son could match the gift. The sultan told Aladdin's mother to go home and not return for three months.

After two months, Aladdin and his mother learned the vizier's son was to marry the princess. Aladdin turned to his lamp for help and asked the genie to bring the vizier's son and the princess to him on their wedding night. When the genie brought the newlyweds in their bed, Aladdin had the genie take the groom outside in the cold. Then he told the princess, "Don't worry. I won't hurt you. You are my wife, promised to me by your father." Aladdin slept soundly, while the princess lay awake. This happened for two more nights, and the family, noticing something was wrong, asked the couple what had happened. The vizier's son said he would rather die than endure another night like the previous ones, and so the couple separated.

Aladdin and his mother awaited the end of the three-month period, and then his mother again appeared before the sultan. The sultan agreed the marriage could take place as soon as she delivered forty basins of gold, carried by forty slaves and led by forty more, all splendidly dressed. When you have a genie, a task like this is no problem. So for the first time, Aladdin made a big request of the genie and sent his mother with the presentation. The sultan was persuaded this time and agreed to the marriage.

Aladdin set to getting ready for his bride. First he outfitted himself royally and then built a marvelous palace and staffed it fully. He asked for enough gold to keep it all running, and his mother set out with a hundred slaves to escort the bride to his new palace. When the princess saw him, she loved him too, and they were very happily married.

The people in the kingdom came to love Aladdin, and the sultan made him a captain in the army. Aladdin was modest and kind, and other than the things he sought to make his wife happy, wanted for little.

Meanwhile the evil sorcerer learned Aladdin lived and had possession of the lamp, so he came to Persia to get the lamp. At the very same time, Aladdin was on an eight-day hunting trip. Disguised as a trader, the magician persuaded the princess to trade the old, beat-up genie lamp for one of his new shiny ones. As soon as he had it he called on the genie to carry him, the palace, and the princess in it away to Africa. Aladdin returned and there was nothing.

The sultan blamed Aladdin for this terrible deed. As he was about to behead him, the kingdom's subjects, who loved Aladdin, came to his rescue. The sultan gave Aladdin forty days to find and return his daughter. Aladdin didn't know what to do, and once more accidentally called forth the ring genie as he prayed. The ring genie couldn't bring back the princess and the palace, but he could take Aladdin right under the princess's windows.

The evil sorcerer had been trying to woo the princess, but she remained loyal to her husband. When she saw Aladdin outside, she brought him into the palace, and they devised a scheme to kill the evil sorcerer. Aladdin gave her a deadly powder to slip into the magician's wine when he came to visit that evening. The princess arrayed herself in her best clothes and jewels. When the magician arrived, she told him she wanted to forget Aladdin and continue with her life. She suggested a toast, and while he went to the wine cellar, she put the powder in her cup. When they toasted, she exchanged her cup for his, and he drained the poisoned wine. The sorcerer fell dead, and the princess let Aladdin into the room. He took the lamp from the magician's vest and ordered the genie to return the palace and them within it home.

All the kingdom celebrated their return, and the sultan welcomed them with ten days of feasting. But their troubles weren't over.

The sorcerer's brother vowed to revenge his death and came looking for Aladdin. He took the identity of a holy woman, Fatima, after killing her, and he went to Aladdin's palace. The princess was immediately taken with Fatima and became very friendly with her. So Fatima moved into the palace, but one day commented to the princess that the palace would be truly beautiful if a hawk's (or any other bird, if you want) egg were hung from the dome in the palace's center hall. The princess passed on her request to Aladdin, who passed it on to the genie. The genie became enraged, because the mythical bird of prey was his master. "Wretch!" he said to Aladdin. The genie threatened to burn the castle and all within it but told Aladdin he wouldn't because he knew the request came from someone else. And then the genie told him about the magician disguised as the holy woman. Feigning a headache, Aladdin called for Fatima to come heal him, and when she came near, he drew a knife and killed her.

Now Aladdin and his wife lived in peace, and when the old sultan died, Aladdin ruled. They lived happily until they died, and their children ruled the kingdom for generations to come.

How to Tell This Story

Aladdin is an old story, and lots of things about it won't make sense to either you or your child. Why does Aladdin never seem to realize the power he has at his fingertips whenever he's in trouble? Why do he and his mother wish for silver to trade for food instead of just wishing for food? Why is the genie so concerned about a hawk?

Still, it's a fun story with an exotic location, magic, and bad guys, and your child will love it. If you want to bring a lesson to the story, try heightening the difference in Aladdin's motivation before and after he falls in love. When he has a goal, nothing can stop him, but before he knew the princess, he didn't have a mission. A lot of people would really drive a genie to distraction with wishes and commands, but Aladdin was different and used his power judiciously. It's fun to think about having a genie, and you might take a story detour while you discuss this with your child.

As in most fairy tales, the princess's only desirable attribute is her beauty. Spend some time adding to her character. Make her eat all her vegetables or score the most goals at soccer or share with her brother, but spend some time on her. Draw out some courtship between Aladdin and the princess. Give her a name, even. What requests do they make of the genie?

Clearly, weddings and women were a little different in Aladdin's day, and you might try changing the story a little bit. Give the princess and the vizier's son a traditional western wedding, but one that's stopped at the last minute. Make the vizier's son cruel and mocking, and describe how the princess appeals to her father to annul the marriage. Try giving the princess a little more spunk and have her refuse to marry the vizier's son because she's already in love with a boy named Aladdin who sings to her nightly. Or leave out the part about the first attempt at marriage and shorten the story. (Leave out the part about the second evil magician and make it shorter still.)

There's a definite charm to this story, and maybe you won't want to change a word, and that's fine too. After all, it is once upon a time.

Androcles and the Lion

Summary

A young slave decided to run away. In the wilderness he befriended a lion by removing a thorn from the lion's paw. Later the slave was recaptured and sentenced to die in the arena facing a wild beast. But it was the same lion. The slave was spared.

The Characters

Androcles: A young slave in ancient Rome.
The lion: Smarter than your average lion.

The Plot

Androcles was your typical slave—abused, overworked, lacking any freedom. He was typical in that he longed for freedom. But Androcles was atypical in that he decided to do something about his predicament: to escape. Androcles reasoned this way: He might die at the hand of some savage animal while wandering the wilderness, but that death would be preferable to the misery he was currently suffering. If captured, he would be killed; but death is preferable to being a slave.

But the wilderness was harsher than he expected. His clothes were torn, his skin cracked and bleeding. He was thirsty and hungry and in pain.

One day he heard a noise coming from a cave. He looked inside the cave and saw a lion. But this lion didn't try to eat Androcles; it didn't even attack him. The lion just moaned and looked forlorn.

Androcles, being brave, went over to the limping lion. Androcles picked up the lion's paw and saw a thorn in the middle of his foot, which Androcles removed. From then on, the lion treated Androcles as if the lion were a puppy dog and Androcles were its master. There was great affection between the two.

Well, one day Androcles had to leave. After all, it's not fitting for a boy to live with a lion forever. Soon after Androcles went on his own, he was captured by the Romans. The penalty for being captured was to be placed in the arena with a lion. In this contest, the lion always won.

But—surprise!—the lion that Androcles was supposed to fight was the lion he had befriended. (The lion had also been caught.) When the lion saw Androcles, he immediately recognized the runaway slave, and hugged the boy. The spectators were amazed that anybody could tame a lion. Both Androcles and the lion were spared.

How to Tell This Story

Most children don't understand the nuances of slavery and don't have the historical background to imbibe the implications of this story. But no matter—it's a fun animal story, and all children like animal stories. "Androcles and the Lion" also has the advantage of being a short tale, which makes it a favorite among parents. You *could* end the story with morals, but the morals of this tale would be lost on many small children. Indeed, if there is a moral worth revealing, it's that animals are mostly nice if you treat them nicely. In other words, don't be cruel to animals.

If you want to make the story longer, you can embellish it by describing the kind of work Androcles had to do, how he lived, how he escaped (inventing a good deal of plot here). Talk a bit about the cave in which the lion lived, the wilderness that Androcles wandered through, and the events that led up to his capture. Invent, too, some dialogue between Androcles and the lion. Kids love to hear animals talk.

Embellish the ending, too. After Androcles was spared, what did he do? Go back to the cave to live with his pet lion?

Become a lion tamer? Eventually become emperor? There are many possibilities.

The Ant and the Cat

Summary

A cat ate an ant. The ant wanted out, but the cat said no. So the ant tickled the cat, which caused the cat to open its mouth, letting the ant out.

The Characters

The cat: Hungry. An ordinary cat, but able to talk (to ants, at least).
The ant: Unwilling to be eaten. Smart and creative.

The Plot

One day a cat was outside prowling around. It came across an ant, which the cat captured and ate.

The ant, when swallowed, wanted out. So the ant said, "Mr. Cat, would you let me out, please?"

The cat said, "No, no, I want to eat you so."

The ant said, "Please let me out."

The cat said, "No, no, I want to eat you so."

The ant said, "Please let me out."

The cat said, "No, no, I want to eat you so."

Finally the ant tickled the cat from the inside, which caused the cat to open its mouth and let the ant out.

How to Tell This Story

Although the dialogue between the ant and the cat seems repetitive, children actually enjoy hearing the same dialogue repeated over and over again. (Right? A three-year-old can watch the same video fifty times before becoming bored with it.) The simplicity and the rhythm make this enjoyable.

In the event that you become tired telling this story, just change the cat to a dog, then a fox, then a giraffe, then a bird, then a horse—you get the idea. A bird? Well, then you talk about how the ant floated to the ground in a breeze. If you change the cat to a fish or frog, be prepared to answer a question about what the ant was doing in the water.

Ashputtel

Summary

Ashputtel is a "Cinderella"-type story. A daughter, shunned by her stepmother and stepsisters, managed to make it to the ball with the help of magic. She enthralled the prince, who wanted to marry her. But the stepmother wanted the prince to marry one of her other—her real—daughters. Eventually, with the help of magic and fate, Ashputtel and the prince fell in love and married.

The Characters

Ashputtel: A Cinderella-like girl. Lovely, simple, and demure. Badly treated by her family and underappreciated. It's her passivity that kept her back. But while she wasn't willing to fight for her rights, Ashputtel was aware of magic in the world around her and used that to her advantage.

The father: A rich man, who loved his daughter, but was not aware of how badly she was treated. He, too, was easily taken advantage of.

Ashputtel's real mother: A kind, beautiful, *and magical* woman, who died all too early. (Her magic is only implied, never stated.) Her only child was Ashputtel.

The stepmother: Crude, rude, and obnoxious, she married the father after his wife passed away. She was nobody's favorite, except for her two daughters, who adored but mostly feared her. She would do anything to better herself.

The prince: Your average prince. Neither ultra-smart, ultra-kind, or ultra-handsome (though he had some of all these qualities.) He had the very desirable quality, however, of being unmarried.

The Plot

This story will sound familiar. A lovely woman, Ashputtel's mother, was dying. Before she died she told Ashputtel how much she loved her and how much she always would. When the mother died, Ashputtel buried her in the woods; every day she brought flowers from her garden to cover the grave.

The following spring, her father remarried an awful woman with two awful daughters. Though these daughters were pretty, they were as mean and rotten as their mother. Ashputtel's stepmother constantly insulted and degraded Ashputtel, calling her a "good-for-nothing." The stepmother made Ashputtel work hard in the kitchen, while her own daughters played; the stepmother took away Ashputtel's clothes and gave the clothes to her daughters; the stepmother made Ashputtel sleep in the hearth on ashes. And that's why she was called Ashputtel—because she was always covered with ashes.

Before Ashputtel's father went to the fair one day he asked his three daughters what they wanted. "Diamonds and emeralds," said the first. "Silk clothes," said the second. Ashputtel said, "Any twig that brushes against your hat as you ride."

The father brought the gifts home and gave Ashputtel her twig, which she planted at her mother's grave. Ashputtel's tears watered the twig, which she visited three times a day, and which soon grew into a beautiful hazel tree. A small bird built a nest in the tree and spent time talking with Ashputtel; the bird brought Ashputtel whatever she needed.

In the fall the king announced that a three-day festival would take place so that the prince, his son, could meet and choose a bride. Ashputtel's stepmother commanded her to polish her stepsisters' shoes for the festival, to clean their dresses, to fix their hair just so. Timidly, Ashputtel asked her stepmother if she, too, could go to the festival. Her stepmother replied that Ashputtel had nothing to wear and couldn't dance and therefore couldn't go. But Ashputtel kept asking. Finally her stepmother threw a hoard of peas into the ash heap and said that if Ashputtel could pick them all up in an hour she could go.

Ashputtel went outside and sang a little song:

> *"Hither, hither, through the sky,*
> *Turtledove and linnet, fly!*
> *Blackbird, thrush, and chaffinch gay,*
> *Hither, hither, haste away!*
> *All sweet birds, come help me quick,*
> *Hasten, hasten—pick, pick, pick!"*

And they did. Mourning doves, turtledoves, finches, bluebirds, every kind of bird came to help Ashputtel. In a flash, they took all the peas from the ash heap and put them in a basin. Ashputtel showed the basin to her stepmother, who called Ashputtel some names and threw twice as many peas into the ash heap and told Ashputtel that she had to get them all out in half an hour. Once again, Ashputtel sang her song for the birds; once again they came to her rescue.

But the stepmother still yelled no. Then she and her daughters got ready for the festival. Ashputtel cried and went into the woods where her mother was buried. There she sang a song:

> *"Green and shadowy hazel tree,*
> *Shed gold and silver over me!"*

Her friend, the original bird, appeared with a gown made of gold and silver and with slippers covered with silk. Ashputtel sped to the festival, where neither her father nor her stepmother recognized her. She had a wonderful time and met the prince, who wanted to marry her. But Ashputtel couldn't stay and slipped away from the prince by hiding in the pigeon house. The prince, of course, had no idea why Ashputtel was so aloof. Ashputtel escaped back to the hazel tree and removed her gown and slippers, which the bird carried away.

The next day Ashputtel returned to the hazel tree and sang for the bird:

> *"Shake, shake, hazel tree,*
> *Gold and silver over me."*

Ashputtel's next gown was even nicer than the previous one. She went to the festival again and enthralled the prince, but just as before, she spirited home before the prince could find out who she was. But this time the prince followed her to the tree. The prince talked to Ashputtel's father, and the father wondered if the girl the prince was talking about could be Ashputtel. He decided it couldn't be.

The next day, Ashputtel went to the festival again and looked even more beautiful than ever. The prince vowed that he wouldn't let her escape. Ashputtel did escape; however, she left her slipper behind.

The king announced that whoever fit into the slipper would get to marry the prince.

Ashputtel's stepsisters tried, but they couldn't fit into the slipper. The older stepsister's foot was too big; her mother told her to cut her big toe off, which she did. Then the shoe fit. The prince and the eldest stepsister rode away together. Af-

ter a while they came to the hazel tree; on the tree branch was
a bird who sang:

> *"Turn again! Turn again! Look to your shoe!*
> *It's a toe's length too small, and was not made for you!*
> *Turn again, Prince. Look elsewhere for thy bride,*
> *A cheat and deceiver sits there at thy side."*

The prince took one look at the sister's foot and knew that she
had tricked him.

The prince went back to town and had the other stepsister
try on the shoe. Too big was her foot! Her mother was enraged and shoved her daughter's foot into the shoe, and finally
it fit. The prince and the stepsister rode into the forest again.
When they passed the hazel tree the little bird sang the same
song:

> *"Turn again, Prince. Look elsewhere for thy bride,*
> *A cheat and deceiver sits there at thy side."*

The prince went back to town and asked the mother if she
had any other daughters. The mother said, "No, except for my
slovenly stepdaughter, Ashputtel, who works in the kitchen."
Despite the mother's harsh words about Ashputtel, the prince
insisted on trying the shoe on Ashputtel. It fit. When the
prince and Ashputtel rode by the hazel tree the bird sang:

> *"Home, now. Home, again. Look at the shoe!*
> *Princess! 'twas I who brought it to you.*
> *Prince! hie away with thy beautiful bride,*
> *She alone is thy loved one and sits at thy side!"*

How to Tell This Story

"Ashputtel," a variation on the "Cinderella" theme, is a
long story. You can shorten it easily by having the three-day

festival became only a one-day event. Alternatively, the story can be lengthened by describing in elaborate detail the costumes, the ballroom, the way the prince looked—everything.

The tree and bird are central to "Ashputtel," but not essential. Replace them with your own brand of magic, if you want: Ashputtel discovered a secret chest in the house; Ashputtel met a kindly witch; Ashputtel found a book of chants and magic that belonged to her mother. Or you can dispense with the magic entirely: Just have Ashputtel become the fastest, most skilled seamstress and shoemaker that ever lived.

The notion of a prince deciding that he's going to marry the most beautiful woman in the land is flattering, but also sexist. There's no reason why you can't modify this fairy tale to require the prince to meet some test proposed by either Ashputtel or the bird. Perhaps Ashputtel decided that she wouldn't marry any old dummy, so she instructed the little bird to fly to the castle and pose a riddle to the prince; if he solved it, then he was destined to find the woman who fit the shoe.

Bastianelo

Summary

A young groom, upset at his wife's and her parents' foolishness on their wedding day, vowed to go out into the world and not return until he found three people sillier than his wife. He quickly found three more foolish people. Satisfied, he went home to his wife. Later they had a son named Bastianelo, and the family lived happily ever after.

The Characters

The bride: Lovable but emotional and let her imagination run away with her.

The bride's mother: Got carried away with her daughter's concerns.

The bride's father: The driving force behind his daughter's personality.

The groom: A trip out into the world showed him his wife wasn't so bad after all.

Fools: A man who tried to collect water in a sieve, a man who didn't know how to get dressed, and a man who couldn't figure out how to get his tall wife to pass beneath a low gate.

The Plot

A young man married the gardener's daughter, and they had a merry wedding party. During the celebration, the wine ran out, and the young bride ran to the cellar to replenish the supply from the wine casks there. As she was filling the casks, she began to think about her future. But she wondered what would happen if she and her husband had a son named Bastianelo and the son died. The thought quite undid her, and she began to cry even as the wine filled the bottle and spilled all over the floor.

In time, her mother missed her and came to see what was wrong. When her distraught daughter shared her concern, she too began to cry. The wine continued to spill all over the cellar. Finally the bride's father came to see what was going on. When he heard the story, he too began to cry as the wine collected around his feet. The groom then came downstairs and was surprised to find everyone standing in wine crying. When he learned the reason why, he vowed to go out into the world and not return until he found three fools greater than the ones in the cellar.

With a change of clothes and some food, he set off in search of fools. After some days, he came upon a man weeping near a well. The man was wet with exertion as well as water, so the groom asked what the matter was. The man said he was having great difficulty filling a pail with water, and then when the groom asked how he was filling the pail, the man replied, "With a sieve." The young man marched to a nearby house, borrowed a bucket, and showed the fool how to fill his bucket from the well. The fool was very grateful, and so was the groom, because he had found one fool greater than his wife.

The young man continued on his way and in the distance saw a man repeatedly jumping from a tree. He was dressed only in a shirt, and as the groom neared, he saw a woman beneath the tree holding some trousers for the man to jump into. They had been doing this for a long time and were quite tired out when the groom drew near. Taking pity on them, the young man showed the pantless man how to get dressed. Then the groom counted to himself, "Two greater fools than my wife."

Not too much longer, the young traveler approached a city, and as he got closer he heard a great noise. A passerby said the noise was from a wedding celebration. The bride was too tall, and riding into the city could not fit under the city gate. The groom and the horse's owner argued about whether it would be better to cut off the horse's legs or the bride's head. This argument was adding to the general wedding uproar. The traveling groom told them he could solve the problem. He pushed the bride so she lay close to the horse's neck and at the same time slapped the horse on the rump. The two neatly fit under the city gate, and the groom counted a third fool to himself.

Satisfied, the groom headed home to his own bride, continued the wedding celebration, and made peace with her and her family. They had a son named Bastianelo, and he didn't die. All three lived long, happy lives.

How to Tell This Story

Add some more fools to this story and make the quest one for four, five, or more fools, and you're got a long story to pass the time. Add foolish actions from modern times or stick to the historical theme of the tale—it's easy enough to think of situations. Your child will want to get into the action too and will come up with plenty of silly situations.

Beauty and the Beast

Summary

This is a story about a prince who got turned into an ugly beast by a witch who didn't like the way he treated women. Not only was the beast ugly, but he was mean. The only way he could be transformed into a man again was to get a woman to fall in love with him. And he had to do this quickly or he would be a beast forever. He captured a beautiful woman, who, although his prisoner, eventually fell in love with him. The beast turned back into a man and he and the woman got married.

The Characters

There are plenty of characters, but only a few are *essential* to the plot. Feel free to include as many subsidiary characters as you want; or exclude as many as you want.

The Beast: An ugly, bitter monster. He lived a life of solitude in a castle, accompanied only by his servants, who once had been people, but were now strange objects.

Beauty: A smart, sensitive, beautiful woman. Although she was beautiful, it's her smartness, her cunning, and her persistence that enable her to be the hero of this story. It's best to give Beauty a name, lest the child you're telling the story to think that her looks are the most important feature. The story then becomes "Mary and the Beast"—or whatever. Use whatever name you want. She was the youngest sister.

Beauty's two older sisters: Unpleasant, unhappy; complainers.
Beauty's brothers: Minor characters. They're in the story to
show that Beauty had a large family.
Beauty's father: A merchant and the victim of bad luck that
caused him to lose his business. Hardworking and caring.

The Plot

For years Beauty's father had been fortunate in business,
able to supply his family with comforts and riches. One day
catastrophe hit: His house burned down and all his ships either sank or were captured by pirates. Despite this sudden
adversity, Beauty remained content; the merchant's other two
daughters turned into complainers.

After a while one of the father's ships reappeared. He set
off on a business trip. All his children told him what presents
they wanted, except for Beauty, who wanted nothing. When
her father said that she must want something, Beauty replied,
"Just a rose, because they're so lovely and none grow around
here."

When the merchant reached the town he found that his former business partners had thought he was dead and divided
his money up among them. He returned home even poorer
than before. On his way back he went though the forest, where
because of the snow he got lost. Eventually he saw a track that
led him to a castle. He spent the night; when he left he picked a
rose from the garden. The Beast appeared and was furious that
the merchant had picked a rose. The Beast told the merchant
that if one of his daughters came to the castle to die in his
place—willingly—the Beast would spare his life.

When the father told Beauty the story, she said she would
go. Her sisters thought she was a fool (the modern expression
would be "jerk"), but Beauty went because she loved her father, who showed her the way to the castle.

The Beast made a room for Beauty. He asked Beauty to
marry him, but Beauty said no.

The castle had many rooms, and they were filled with monkeys and other fun things that Beauty played with. Day after day, the Beast asked Beauty to marry him, but her answer was always the same: "No."

Beauty got everything she wanted. Still, she missed her father, family, and friends. The Beast saw this unhappiness in her and said that she could return to her family for two months. To return to the Beast's castle, the Beast gave Beauty a magic ring and told her that on the night before she was to come back to the castle all she had to do was twist the ring twice. The Beast told Beauty that she could take gold, jewels, silver, or anything she wanted back to her family as presents. On the morning Beauty was to leave for her visit, she awoke in her father's house.

One night, weeks before Beauty was to return to the castle, she looked into the stone on the ring the Beast had given to her. In the stone she saw the Beast's image—and he was dying. Beauty panicked and turned the ring twice—in an instant she was back at the castle. She looked for the Beast, and finally found him in the garden. Beauty cried because she found him, dying, she thought, in the garden. The Beast opened his eyes: "Do you really care for me, even though I am so ugly?"

"Yes, Beast, I do. I want to marry you."

And then there was a brilliant light and the Beast turned into a handsome prince. Beauty's words had broken the spell of a powerful witch, who had turned this prince into a Beast. It was a spell that could be broken only if a beautiful woman told the Beast she loved him.

Beauty and the Beast were married.

How to Tell This Story

There's no reason why only a beautiful woman can break the spell—it could be a smart woman, or, even better, a woman who takes naps or goes to sleep on time.

But wait! Where are Mrs. Potts, Lumiere, and Cogsworth? Where are Chip and Gaston? If you've seen the Disney movie *Beauty and the Beast*, the traditional version will seem a little thin to you. Feel free to introduce any characters from the movie, or keep the story as short as it is in the original.

Children are going to be interested in what Beauty and the Beast looked like. They're also going to wonder about the castle, and the magical things and creatures in the castle. You could tell your audience what these things looked like, or you could have the child tell you.

Blue Beard

Summary

A wealthy man with a hideous blue beard couldn't find a wife he could trust with his secret and had to kill each wife as soon as he married her because she might betray him. His last wife was different, and survived by her wits when she persuaded Blue Beard to allow her to live long enough to say her prayers. All the while she knew her two brothers were on their way to her rescue. They killed the wicked husband and saved their sister.

While a classic tale, "Blue Beard" is a horror story. It may not be suitable for many toddlers. But the story can be modified in many ways to de-horrify it.

The Characters

Blue Beard: He had the misfortune of growing blue whiskers before the Smurfs made the color popular. He was tremendously wealthy, with city and country homes, both furnished with fine goods. His coaches were even gilded.

Women were repulsed by him. Did the taunts and rejection of women make him evil or was it just a part of his makeup?

The older sister, Anne: She wouldn't marry Blue Beard, but she did what she could to help her younger sister. She had sharp vision.

The younger sister: Blue Beard's wealth made him a little more desirable to her, although she didn't know why he had such a high wife turnover. Blue Beard sentenced her to death when she disobeyed him.

The two brothers: Carried sharp swords they put to good use.

The Plot

Blue Beard wanted a new wife. No one knew what had happened to his last one, or the one before her, or the several before her, so marriageable women were afraid of him. Well, there was that and the fact that they found his blue whiskers repulsive. So Blue Beard had trouble meeting women.

At his town home, his neighbor was a woman with two attractive and single daughters and two sons. Blue Beard wanted to marry either one of the beautiful girls, but neither wanted him, and so they pushed him back and forth between them. To impress the girls, he invited them and their mother to accompany him and a party of other people to his country home for a week. They enjoyed a week of fun—music, food, dancing, hunting, fishing, every sort of entertainment. As the week passed, the younger sister began to think maybe Blue Beard wasn't such a bad fellow after all. She consented to marry him.

Soon Blue Beard told his new wife that business would take him away for six weeks and she should invite her friends and relatives to go with her to their country home for a holiday. He gave her keys to the home's wardrobes where he kept his gold and silver plates, his money, and his jewels, a key to all the apartments in the home, and a little key to a closet on the ground floor. Blue Beard warned his wife not to open the closet or he would be very angry. Then he left.

The wife's friends and sister came to visit as soon as her husband left, and they ran all through the house examining all the riches within. But the wife couldn't stop thinking about the forbidden closet, and she left her company to go open the closet. She paused before she opened it, but then she couldn't resist and twisted the key in the lock. Behind the closet door she found a dark room full of dead women, Blue Beard's former wives. In her shock, she dropped the key on the bloody floor. Quickly, she picked up the key, locked the door, and ran upstairs to be alone in her room.

The key had a bloodstain on it she couldn't remove no matter how she rubbed and scrubbed, and to her dismay, Blue Beard returned that very evening. In the morning he asked for the keys and noticed she had kept back the closet key. He sent her to get it, and when she gave it to him, he asked how it had become bloodstained. Although his wife denied she had been in the closet, Blue Beard knew she had seen the bodies and told her she must take her place among them. No matter how his wife begged, Blue Beard wouldn't show mercy. Finally he agreed to give her fifteen minutes to say her prayers.

She went to her room and immediately called her sister, Anne, to come to her. She told Anne to go to the top of the tower and keep watch for their brothers, who were expected to arrive that day. Again and again the wife asked Anne if she saw their brothers coming, but there was no sign. Blue Beard bellowed for his wife to come to him. Still Anne saw nothing. Then just before the wife went down to Blue Beard, Anne saw two horsemen in the distance, and she signaled for them to hurry.

The wife crumpled at Blue Beard's feet and again begged for mercy, but he hauled her up by her hair and was just about to cut off her head when the brothers arrived, drew their swords, and slew Blue Beard.

The wife inherited Blue Beard's fortune and split it with her sister and brothers. She herself married a fine gentleman and tried to forget her time with Blue Beard.

and you don't really have to pee, then when you do really have to pee, Mommy and Daddy might not come because they don't believe you and you'll end up with very wet sheets.

This is a simple, short story, and its brevity can be a blessing at bedtime. Still, there are ways to lengthen it, to make it more interesting. There's always the shepherd's house, the shepherd's garden, the shepherd's family to describe.

The Bremen Town Musicians

Summary

This is a story about four animals so old that they were put out to pasture by their masters. The donkey, the leader of the pack, decided to go to Bremen, a musical town, to become a musician, for lack of anything else to do. En route, the animals scared away some robbers, took their food, and discovered that they were not so old and weak after all.

The Characters

The characters are an old donkey, an old dog, an old rooster, and an old cat. They have all been made to believe that they are too old to be of value. But they discovered that age was a mental issue, and in fact they were as young as they wanted to be.

The Plot

A donkey had been faithful to his master for years, hauling and pulling. But when the donkey became too old, the master decided that it was too expensive to feed the donkey, and sent him away. The donkey decided to go to Bremen, a town where everyone played music. The donkey wanted to become a musician.

On the way he saw an old dog, panting. The dog, because he could no longer hunt, had been discarded by his master. So the donkey asked the dog if he wanted to go to Bremen town, too. The donkey said that he would play the guitar and the dog could play drums.

The donkey and dog found a cat along the road. The cat had a sad face. Because he could no longer catch mice, the cat's owner had sent him away. The donkey said to the cat, "Come with us to Bremen town. You can be a singer; we're all going to be musicians!"

After another mile, the trio came upon a rooster, who had a sorry tale to tell: His master was going to turn the rooster into stew. "Oh no!" said the dog. "Come with us to Bremen. You can sing, too!"

So the four animals continued on their journey. Soon it became dark and they needed a place to stay. They saw a house with people inside. The donkey, the tallest, looked inside and saw a table filled with food. "But there are robbers at the table," he warned his compatriots.

The animals agreed that it would be wonderful if they could be inside where it was warm, and have that food. The donkey and the dog and the cat and the rooster talked and formed a plan. The donkey leaned with his hooves against the window. The dog climbed on top of the donkey, the cat on top of the dog, and the rooster on top of the cat. They brayed and howled and meowed and clacked and made music. So much music that it scared away the robbers. The animals went inside and enjoyed a feast. Afterward, they each slept the night in a comfortable bed.

The robbers, meanwhile, decided to attack back. The head robber sneaked inside. He carried a burning match for light. Tiptoeing around the kitchen, he saw the cat's eyes, and thinking they were coals, put the match to them. The cat was angry—he scratched and hollered and spat. The robber ran for the door. The dog, who had been awakened by the noise, bit the robber on the leg. On his way out, the donkey kicked him on the bottom. And the rooster began yelling, "Cock-a-doodle-doo!"

The robber ran as fast as he could away from the house. He told his comrades, "The house has an evil witch that spits. A man with a knife stabbed me in the legs, a monster with a club hit me, and on the roof there's a judge yelling, 'Hang the thieves! Hang the thieves!' I'm lucky to have made it out with my life."

How to Tell This Story

This story, I've found, is just the right length, has just the right mixture of animals and people, and has enough action that it doesn't need any changes. Of course, there is a moral: You're only as old as you feel; even old, tired animals and people can accomplish great things. But it's unlikely that a small child will be able to relate to any of these morals. Of course, there is one other message that you can get across: You can do anything if you try.

Can you sing? Even if you can't, go ahead and sing the song that the animals would sing. Something like:

> We're going to Bremen town
> All of us a-going to that town
> We're a donkey, and a dog, and a cat, and a rooster.

It doesn't matter that the song has no rhythm or rhyme—your child will like it anyway.

Br'er Rabbit and the Tar Baby

Summary

This is one of the adventures of Br'er Rabbit; there are many others. Br'er Fox made a Tar Baby—a baby rabbit fashioned out of tar—as a trap to capture Br'er Rabbit. ("Br'er" is a dialect pronunciation of "brother.") Br'er Rabbit came along and got stuck to the tar rabbit. Br'er Fox then told Br'er Rabbit that Br'er Rabbit was going to be supper. Br'er Rabbit tricked Br'er Fox into getting Br'er Rabbit free from the tar rabbit.

The Characters

Br'er Fox: A cunning fox. Sort of a southeastern version of Coyote in the Roadrunner cartoons. But, clever and self-confident as the fox was, Br'er Rabbit was smarter.

Br'er Rabbit: A rabbit that lived around the briar patch. He and Br'er Fox didn't get along, especially because Br'er Fox wanted to eat him.

The Plot

Br'er Fox mixed some tar and turpentine to make a baby rabbit out of tar, which he placed in the middle of the road. Along came Br'er Rabbit—hippity, hop, hippity, hop—and saw the tar baby. Br'er Rabbit tried to talk to the tar baby, but it wouldn't reply. He asked the tar baby if it was sick; he shouted at the tar baby: *"Are you deaf?"* Finally, Br'er Rabbit grabbed the tar baby and shook it, because he thought that the tar baby was just making fun of him. Well, when he grabbed the tar baby, he got stuck.

Then Br'er Fox emerged from hiding. He told Br'er Rabbit

that Br'er Rabbit was going to become dinner. Br'er Fox was especially gleeful about this occasion, because for the longest time Br'er Rabbit had been taunting him, making fun of Br'er Fox's inability to catch Br'er Rabbit, just as Coyote could never catch the Roadrunner. Now the tables were turned.

Br'er Fox told Br'er Rabbit that he was going to roast him. Br'er Rabbit said that he didn't care, just as long as Br'er Fox didn't throw him in the briar patch—the thorns were bound to hurt!

Br'er Fox said he was going to hang Br'er Rabbit, because making a fire was too much work. Br'er Rabbit said, "Okay, just as long as you don't throw me in the briar patch."

Then Br'er Fox said that he didn't have any rope for hanging, but would drown Br'er Rabbit. To which Br'er Rabbit replied, "That's okay with me, as long as you don't throw me in the briar patch." Br'er Fox said that the creek was low and he couldn't drown Br'er Rabbit, so he would have to skin him. "Okay, skin me," said Br'er Rabbit. "Just don't throw me in the briar patch."

Well, Br'er Fox wanted to hurt Br'er Rabbit just as much as he wanted to eat him. So he picked up Br'er Rabbit and flung him into the briar patch. As it happened, the thorns and prickly bushes cut Br'er Rabbit loose from the tar baby. Br'er Rabbit had tricked Br'er Fox! Br'er Rabbit was free.

How to Tell This Story

There are some seemingly scary moments in "Br'er Rabbit," but it's not all that scary to most children. You can even add other techniques that Br'er Fox might use to munch on Br'er Rabbit.

Chicken Licken

Summary

This is the story of Chicken Licken and her friends, who embark on a quest to warn the king that the sky is falling. None of the animals except Chicken Licken claim to have seen the sky fall themselves; they merely take Chicken Licken's word for it. They all get so worked up over their mission that when a fox tells them to come into his den for protection from the falling sky, they do so and are eaten.

The Characters

Chicken Licken: Believed that the sky was falling. A chicken with too vivid an imagination.

Henny Penny, Cocky Locky, Ducky Daddles, Turkey Lurkey, and Goosey Loosey: All as gullible as one can get.

Foxy Woxy: A sly fox, and clearly much smarter than the rest, though he didn't have to be very smart to outwit them.

The Plot

Chicken Licken believed the sky was falling because an acorn fell on her head. So she embarked on a journey to warn the king.

On her way she met a cast of other animals (in order): Henny Penny, Cocky Locky, Ducky Daddles, Turkey Lurkey, and Goosey Loosey. Each time the new animals asked, "Good morning, Chicken Licken. Where are you going?" Chicken Licken said the sky was falling and answered the inevitable question "How do you know the sky is falling?" with the response: "I saw it with my own eyes, heard it with my own ears, and felt a piece of the sky fall on my head." As new animals were added to the parade, each said, "I know because [the previous animal] told me," ending with Henny Penny, who said, "Chicken Licken told me."

Finally they met Foxy Woxy, who suggested that they wait in his den, and said that he would tell the king. Foxy Woxy then ate them all.

How to Tell This Story

Be sure to repeat the dialogue at each meeting. The more repetitious the better. (Do melodies really put children to sleep? Here's your chance to find out.) When Turkey Lurkey encounters the parade, she should say, "Good morning, Chicken Licken, Goosey Loosey . . ." When asked how they know the sky is falling, each animal replies that the previous animal told them, until they come to Chicken Licken.

Do you think the sky is falling when an acorn falls? The answer is always no. So you can be reassured that your children are smarter than Chicken Licken and her friends. If your audience likes discussing stories, this is a good one to talk about. Otherwise, it's simply a good tale in itself.

The Elves and the Shoemaker

Summary

This is a story about a poor shoemaker who ran out of material from which to makes shoes. Magically, new shoes appeared in his shop overnight. This happened again and again. When the shoemaker and his wife stayed awake all night to see what was up, they found two naked elves working hard. The shoemaker decided to make the elves clothes. The elves put on the clothes, and then were never seen again. But the shoemaker was left with good luck.

The Characters

The shoemaker: An elderly, kindly man, having bad luck lately. His business wasn't going well, through no fault of his own. He couldn't make shoes to sell because he couldn't afford material to make the shoes.

The shoemaker's wife: Also a kindly person. She helped the shoemaker sell shoes.

The elves: Tiny beings with implied magical powers and fantastic shoemaking skills. It's unclear how they came to know about the shoemaker's problems. The elves wore no clothing.

The customers: A small cast of characters who would have liked to buy shoes from the shoemaker, if only he had had something to offer.

The Plot

The shoemaker became poorer and poorer over the years. Now he only had enough leather to make one more pair of shoes.

He planned to do the best he could with the material at hand, and he cut a pattern. When he got up in the morning, the shoes were finished—and perfect, too.

A customer walked into the shop and bought the shoes. With the money, the shoemaker purchased material for two more pairs of shoes. He cut patterns for those shoes, and went to sleep, planning on sewing the shoes in the morning.

In the morning, there were two more beautiful pairs of shoes made. The shoemaker sold the shoes at a good price. Now the shoemaker had money to buy material for four pairs of shoes.

Next morning, there were four finished pairs of shoes—and they were bought right away.

The process continued, and in short order, the shoemaker became a wealthy man.

One evening the shoemaker and his wife decided to stay awake to see how this was happening. They saw two elves, hard at work. But the elves wore no clothes. As soon as the elves were finished they ran away.

So the shoemaker and his wife made the elves some clothes to thank them. The shoemaker was concerned that the elves were outside in the cold with no clothes. The shoemaker and his wife worked night and day and made tiny shirts, pants, caps, coats, and socks.

When the elves returned, instead of cuttings for shoes they found clothes. They put on the clothes with delight and sang a song: "Now that we're boys so fine and neat/Why cobble more for others' feet?"

The elves never returned, but the shoemaker continued to prosper and had good luck in everything he did.

How to Tell This Story

Your child may be curious about what the shoes looked like. Probably not like Nikes, or Velcro Stride Rites. But they might have been children's shoes!

Also it's possible that the shoemaker let the process continue for a few days or months before staying up to find out what was happening. Perhaps the shoemaker left out some cookies in the interim. One version of the fairy tale has the shoemaker staying up not long before Christmas and leaving the clothes out on Christmas eve.

Add dialogue between the shoemaker and his wife. You might also be inclined to mention the shoemaker's children—naturally, they were grown up and living in another village, too far away to help their parents. Then there's the matter of the elves dancing about the shoemaker's shop: I imagine it could have been quite a scene.

You can also make up a lot about the elves. What did they look like? Where did they come from? What did the clothing the shoemaker and his wife made look like? Teeny-tiny socks, itsy-bitsy shirts, eensy-weensy pants—children love to hear about miniaturized things. And they love to hear their parents' voices.

This isn't a story you have to worry about shortening; it passes quickly.

The Emperor's New Clothes

Summary

"The Emperor's New Clothes" takes place in an imaginary kingdom. The emperor had more clothes than Imelda Marcos had shoes. Clothes, the emperor thought, made him what he was. So the emperor was easily conned by two strangers who offered to stitch him the most beautiful clothes in the world, and clothes with a magical quality—they would be invisible to fools. When the clothes were finished (at great cost to the emperor), the emperor couldn't see them, but he was too image-conscious to admit that the clothes were invisible to him because he was a dolt. In fact, nobody in the kingdom would admit that he or she saw no clothes. Would you? Finally, during a parade, a little boy yelled out, "The emperor has no clothes!" After a couple moments, everyone else, including the emperor, realized the truth.

The Characters

The emperor: Can also be called a king, if that speeds things up. A good emperor, but because he was so often flattered by subjects seeking favors, he grew vain, self-centered, and too proud to admit mistakes. Because he paid so much attention to his clothes, he neglected to pay attention to the world around him.

Two crooks: Swindlers, con artists, bad men. In another era, they'd be playing three-card monte.

The townspeople: Loved their emperor and were too worried about being thought of as fools to state their real opinions.

The emperor's assistants: Too patronizing to be helpful.

The little boy (or little girl) who saw the truth: The story's hero.

The Plot

The story can open any number of ways. You could introduce the emperor by talking about his clothes, or you could talk about the emperor's great horsemanship, the dogs he owned, all sorts of things to emphasize the emperor's niceness. People liked this emperor, in contrast to the emperors and kings in other fairy tales, who are frequently evil.

But his clothes. His clothes were fantastic—even nicer-looking than Mommy's and Daddy's clothes. Even nicer than the President's. And the emperor has so many—one set of clothes for each day of the year, and maybe even two sets. Nobody had ever counted—few of the kingdom's subjects could count that high. Can you?

The emperor liked to walk among his subjects. One day he was approached by two men (the emperor didn't know they were crooks) who offered to make him the most beautiful clothes in the world. And these clothes, the swindlers said, would also have a magical quality—they would be invisible to fools and idiots. So the emperor would be able to tell who, among his subjects and staff, were fools.

The emperor paid the swindlers handsomely to make his clothes. He also bought the most expensive silk and gold thread with which the swindlers were supposed to make the clothes. (They sold the silk and thread to get even richer at the emperor's expense.)

The swindlers took a long time to make the clothes; that's because they had no intention of sewing anything. When the emperor asked how his new clothes were coming along, the swindlers replied, "Fine, magnificently; they'll be ready in no time." But the emperor grew impatient, and one day, along with his most trusted assistant, he walked unannounced into the swindlers' house to see the progress of his clothes.

"Look, see—see how wonderful they are becoming!" one of the swindlers said.

And the emperor and his assistant nodded and replied, "Yes, the clothes are indeed beautiful!" The emperor didn't want anybody to know he couldn't see the clothes and was therefore a fool. And the emperor's trusted assistant wouldn't admit the truth either, because nobody should think that an emperor's assistant is a fool.

In another week, the swindlers delivered the emperor's new clothes. "See how great they are," the swindlers said.

"Yes," replied the emperor, and "Yes," replied the emperor's assistants. The emperor decided to have a parade that day to show off his new clothes.

There were no new clothes, really, so the emperor was parading in the nude. But because everybody in the kingdom had heard about the new clothes and because nobody wanted to be called a fool, everyone oohed and aahed over the emperor's new clothes.

Except one little boy, who, though he had heard about the clothes, believed his eyes and not his ears. The little boy (or little girl) shouted, "But the emperor has no clothes!"

"Hush," said the boy's mother. But the boy's truth rang loudly, and everybody else watching the parade said, "The emperor has no clothes." At that moment, the emperor realized that he had been taken advantage of, but he had no choice except to continue marching naked.

How to Tell This Story

There are several good lessons here, and you may want to tell the story to emphasize these lessons. Lesson one: Don't believe what everybody tells you. Lesson two: Trust what you see, trust your own eyes. Lesson three: Nothing bad happens to you when you tell the truth. Lesson four: Put on your clothes before going outside. (A simpler, more immediate lesson.)

This story can be told very quickly; under a minute isn't too fast.

Or you can embellish it: Take a minute to describe each of the emperor's sets of clothes. That's 365 minutes, or a little over six hours.

"The Emperor's New Clothes" can be told simply as a fun story, which it is. But if you want to use it to illustrate lessons, then it's worthwhile to embellish the emperor's and the little boy's characters. The emperor was very nice, but too trusting. He was generous, but not wise.

The little boy was too innocent to realize the implications of telling adults what they want to hear rather than the truth. Although the emperor was mightily embarrassed when he realized he was parading naked, he preferred knowing the truth.

What happened to the swindlers? Well, the answer is not part of the original story, but if you want you can make up something: They were forced to parade through the town square in their underwear; they were run out of town; they were made to sew clothes for everyone in the kingdom.

In some versions of the story, the emperor was a bad ruler: vain, shallow, and unconcerned about his subjects, who were all afraid of him. The swindlers were actually the good guys, in a sense, because they were out to prove conclusively that the emperor had no judgment and was unfit to rule. When the emperor ordered his subjects to praise his new clothes, they did so out of terror. Only one little boy, too young to understand the consequences, spoke out. After that, everyone else was free to do the same. The emperor was quickly deposed as his subjects all realized that they didn't have to put up with that fool anymore.

The Fairy Wife

Summary

A Greek folk tale about a marriage between a mortal and a fairy. A goatherd fell in love with a fairy and managed to capture her when she dropped her handkerchief. He married her and they had a daughter, but the fairy was always unhappy. One day she managed to get her handkerchief back and returned to her fairy sisters. On her fifteenth birthday, the daughter also went to live with the fairies. The goatherd wandered the earth all alone seeking his wife and child and singing a song asking them to return.

The Characters

Demetros: The goatherd. He didn't listen to his mother, who warned him to stay away from fairies.

His mother: She knew fairies were trouble.

Katena: She was the most graceful and beautiful of fairies, and she certainly didn't want to marry a goatherd. Whoever controlled her handkerchief controlled her, and Demetros accidentally latched onto it as he tried to grab her.

Neraidokoretso: Her name means "fairy child." She never formed any attachment to her grandmother or father.

The Plot

A lonely goatherd, Demetros, lived with his mother. One evening after he drove the goats home, he had to go for water because his mother was ill. He set off for the Fairy Spring, where the citizens often spotted fairies.

When he arrived, three girls were sitting in the moonlight near the spring, but Demetros thought nothing of it, assuming they were shepherdesses. As a rooster crowed at the coming dawn, the girls rose, joined hands, and danced westward, until they disappeared in a puff of smoke. Demetros watched mesmerized, and then he stumbled home but told no one what he had seen. That night he went again and watched six girls dance in the moonlight. When his mother noticed his distraction, he told her what he had seen. She warned him to stay away from the fairies, but he returned anyway on the third night, when he watched nine fairies dance and then disappear. He was so distracted he didn't even remember to get water, and his mother once more warned him to stay away. The coming full moon would render the fairies even more powerful.

That night the fairies were at the spring, and a new one even more beautiful and graceful than the rest had joined the nine. They sang a lovely song about freedom, riding the winds, and being happy, then they lured Demetros off to the west with them. He forgot his mother and the goats and followed. The most beautiful fairy danced near him, and he reached out to catch her, but caught only her handkerchief. The dance ended and all the fairies ran away but for the one he sought. She sank in despair and was forced to follow Demetros. She told him he had robbed her of her happiness.

Demetros tucked the handkerchief into his belt and walked toward home. The fairy Katena followed, weeping all the way. When he got home, his mother welcomed Demetros and his wife. She took the handkerchief and locked it in a box where the fairy couldn't get to it. (A fairy is bound to remain wherever her handkerchief is kept.) Katena spent her time embroidering, spinning, and sewing. She made lovely clothes for herself, her mother-in-law, and her daughter, Neraidokoretso, who came along shortly. Katena was never happy, though, and that concerned Demetros. Their daughter was every bit the fairy child, and each day she grew more like her mother.

Seven years after Demetros had captured Katena, his mother left home to visit some relatives on St. Konstantinos Day. Demetros was surprised when Katena asked him to take her dancing in the village. She told him to bring her a pretty dress and her best handkerchief. Demetros grabbed the first dress he found, but he had to search through his mother's belongings to find the handkerchief locked away in a box. He tucked the handkerchief in his belt, and he, Katena, and Neraidokoretso set out for the festival. Demetros and Katena danced on the village green with other dancers, but then came a dance where couples danced in pairs, not in a great circle. Demetros and Katena faced one another holding a handkerchief stretched between them. Katena's turn came to lead the dance, and Demetros dropped his corner of the handkerchief. Katena danced away, whirled into the sky, and disappeared. Demetros was crushed, and he and Neraidokoretso returned home.

Demetros and his mother thought the girl would be very unhappy without her mother, but she thrived. Each day she disappeared into the hills and came home happy and tired. One day, Demetros followed her and saw her go to the Fairy Spring, where she held her arms to the sky as a white mist descended. Then he knew she went there to see her mother. On her fifteenth birthday, Neraidokoretso went to the spring for the last time. When she held up her arms, the mist surrounded her and lifted her away to be with her mother.

Demetros gave up goatherding and took to wandering the woods and hills looking for his wife and daughter. He sang a little song to entice them, but they never came.

How to Tell This Story

This melancholy story might seem too sad to tell, but give it a try. If you think your child might be disturbed by it, then try an alternative ending. Build the relationship between Demetros and Neraidokoretso. Maybe Demetros was able to win Katena's love by learning how to dance to please her. When she saw how hard he tried to please her, her fairy heart softened. Perhaps Demetros could visit fairyland on week-ends. Draw the story out; make Katena start to miss Demetros and return to visit. Or maybe this old tale can just parallel modern reality: Neraidokoretso splits her time between her parents because she loved them both so much. Maybe Demetros could change into a fairy.

The Fir Tree

Summary

This is a sad tale of a fir tree that spent so much of its life wishing to be something else somewhere else that it didn't enjoy its life. After a brief time of happiness as a Christmas tree, it was tossed away and eventually burned. You'll be using live Christmas trees with root balls after your child hears this tale.

The Characters

The fir tree: Never content. It wanted to be a towering tree when it was only a sapling, a ship's mast when it could enjoy the summer forest.

Assorted animals: They told the fir tree about the sights of the world, and it longed to see them for itself.

A large family: They didn't really appreciate their Christmas tree, and after a few days tossed it into the garret.

The Plot

As the smallest tree in a forest of pines and firs, the young fir sapling wanted nothing more than to grow big and tall, because it didn't enjoy the sights, sounds, and feelings of being young. After three years, some trees around it were cut and hauled away. Later that year, the swallows and storks told the fir tree the felled trees became ships' masts and had great adventures. The fir tree longed to go to sea. That winter, some people came into the forest to cut Christmas trees, but didn't choose the fir tree. The sparrows described the glory of a Christmas tree, how people decorated it and honored it (although they didn't know what happened to the trees after they were decorated). Of course, then the fir tree wanted to be a Christmas tree and didn't appreciate the glorious winter.

All the time the fir tree was wishing for a new life, the air, sunlight, dew, and breeze warned it to enjoy the moment and savor life. But it didn't listen.

The next winter, the fir tree was chosen for a Christmas tree. The sharp ax hurt, and now the fir tree was unhappy at leaving its fine forest home. After an uncomfortable journey, the fir tree was erected in a large and beautifully furnished hall. It thought things were looking up when servants placed its trunk in a tub of sand and decorated it gaily. They hung bags of candies from its branches, fastened candles to it, and nestled presents beneath it. The fir tree wore a golden star on its top, and thoroughly enjoyed itself all evening as the candles were lit and then the children rushed in to pluck all the gifts from its branches. As the candles burned down, it began to feel ignored, but then enjoyed listening to a man tell the children the story of Humpty Dumpty, who fell downstairs but married a princess. The tree couldn't wait until the next day, when it would all begin again. He wished he could marry a princess like Humpty Dumpty and was optimistic it could happen to him too. He remembered a cute tree from the forest.

But in the morning, the servants took the tree and dragged it to a garret, where they tossed it on the floor in a corner. The fir tree thought it was being left there until spring, when it would be replanted. It was lonely even with these pleasant thoughts and longed to be back in the forest with the animals, sunshine, and snow. When some mice found the garret, the fir tree was happy for the company. They talked about where they were from, and the mice envied the fir tree's adventures and happiness, and it had to agree life had been good in the forest. Then the fir tree told the mice of its grandest moment as a Christmas tree and shared the story of Humpty Dumpty. More mice came to visit, and then a few rats, but the rats weren't impressed, and the mice soon lost interest. The fir tree was left alone.

When the spring came, the fir tree was dragged into the yard. It discovered its branches were withered and yellow, and the children playing in the yard called it ugly. Then the fir tree felt very sad that it hadn't enjoyed its life more, always wishing for something different. A boy chopped the tree into pieces and burned it. As the tree burned, it sighed at what happiness it had ignored, and each sigh made a loud popping noise.

How to Tell This Story

This sad story has a place in your repertoire, probably when your child is making you crazy wishing for a birthday to come about, or a vacation, or a visit from the grandparents. You'll know when to use it, and you can expect a change in behavior. For a few days, anyway.

Add some characters to the beginning of the tale. Trees got taken away to become all sorts of products, each of which sounded terribly exciting to the fir tree. Newspapers, books, crates, and furniture—what products can your child think of?

The Christmas in this story was an old fashioned one, so try to heighten the differences between then and now. Before electric lights, people lit candles on the tree's branches, a dangerous practice that often led to fires. And before gifts became so ambitious, children used to be happy to retrieve fruits, nuts, and sweets from among the tree's branches. If you don't want to research the history of Christmas celebrations, try describing one from your childhood, which will seem like ancient times to your child. Alternatively, describe one of your family's Christmases to help your child relate better.

The Fisherman and His Wife

Summary

A poor fisherman found a magic flounder to grant his humble wishes. First his wife wished for a cottage to replace their poor shack. Unfortunately, the wife wasn't satisfied and kept making progressively grander wishes until she asked to be made God. Then they ended up in their original shack.

The Characters

An enchanted flounder: A prince turned into a fish by a witch's spell. He never passed judgment about the wishes; he just granted them impassively.
A fisherman: A humble man who couldn't say no to his wife.
The fisherman's wife: A shrew who was never happy.

The Plot

One day a poor fisherman caught a flounder, a large one who could speak. The flounder told him he was an enchanted prince, which would make him taste really bad, so the fisherman agreed to let him go. When he arrived home empty-handed, his wife scolded him for releasing the fish without asking anything in return. She ordered him to return to the place where he had caught the fish and ask for a nice cottage. So the fisherman went to the sea and said,

> *"Flounder, Flounder in the sea*
> *Will you please listen to me?*
> *My wife sends me with a wish*
> *To ask of my princely fish."*

The flounder surfaced and asked the fisherman what he wanted. The fisherman apologized for bothering him and then told the fish about the wish for a cottage. The flounder told him his wife had her wish, and when the fisherman got home, he saw it was true. His wife showed him all around the sweet cottage, which was well furnished and had a yard full of chickens and ducks and even a lush garden. The fisherman said they would live very happily this way, but his wife only said, "We'll see about that." After a week, the wife seemed unhappy and told her husband the cottage was too small and she wanted a big stone castle.

The fisherman trudged to the sea once more, spoke, and the flounder granted the wish. His wife was happy for a day. Then she asked to be queen. The fisherman made the request of the flounder, and this wish came true too. But as soon as the fisherman got home, his wife demanded he return to the sea and ask that she be made emperor. He did, and it happened. But again when he got home his wife was unhappy and sent him back to the sea to have her made Pope. And that happened too. When he got home, it was late, so they went to bed. The wife slept poorly and in the morning asked her husband to go to the sea and ask the flounder to make her Lord of the Universe. When her husband balked, she went into a rage, so he obeyed her.

The flounder put them back in the old hovel. The fisherman and his wife still live there today.

How to Tell This Story

The wife got progressively more demanding and impatient each time she got what she wanted. The more she got, the more unhappy she became. Describe this in great detail and act it out. She can have tantrums like a willful child. Stamp your feet, wave your arms about in the air, raise your voice, and have fun.

Describe each new setting in great detail. What was in

the cottage? The castle? How is an emperor's home different from a king's? How did the wife's appearance change
each time? Speed up your speech each time the wife de-
mands something new to heighten the point that she was
not satisfied for long with each gift she received. When you
get to the end, you're breathless when you say they went
back to their old hovel. Don't pass up the opportunity to
make the point that sometimes people need someone to say
"NO."

The Fox and the Grapes

Summary

Describing the plot takes as long as telling the whole story,
but here goes: A Fox was trying to jump to get some grapes.
He couldn't reach them. Finally he gave up and said, "I didn't
want those grapes anyway; they're sour."

The Characters

The fox: Hungry.
The grapes: Not to be eaten.

The Plot

A fox who was really hungry saw some grapes hanging
from the top of a grapevine. The fox said to himself, "Those
grapes look so sweet and delicious." He jumped up to try to
get them, but couldn't.

After trying several times, the fox gave up and said,
"Those grapes were too sour anyway."

How to Tell This Story

When you're looking for a bedtime story, there's virtue in brevity. This story can be told in a couple of sentences. Adding the moral is optional, but the moral goes like this: Just because you can't have something doesn't make it bad, or sour. (You probably didn't know that.) To add some frills to the story you can talk about the fox's fur, about the grapes (were they green or purple?), about the meadow, about the other animals around. You can even introduce other creatures who either tell the fox to work harder, or perhaps encourage him to give up. Establishing a dialogue among animals always makes a hit with children.

The Frog Prince

Summary

A prince who has been turned into a frog by a curse was changed back to a prince by a princess, whom the frog then married.

The Characters

The frog: An enchanted prince.
The princess: A beautiful but slightly spoiled child; she loved to play with her golden ball near the well.
The king: Fair and just; he made the princess keep her promise to the frog.

The Plot

The beautiful princess was playing with her golden ball near the well when she accidentally knocked the golden ball into the well. She was beside herself with grief. The frog offered to bring her the ball, but only if she promised to make him her companion. She agreed, but after the frog rescued her ball she ran to the castle, leaving the frog alone.

The frog did not give up, however, and went to the castle to claim his due. The king forced the princess to keep her promise to the frog. She had to allow the frog to eat off her plate, sit by her side, and sleep in her bed! In the beginning, she hated this. But she was won over by the frog's kindness and gentle manner. One day she kissed the frog. The frog turned into a handsome prince, released by the beautiful princess from a witch's curse. They married and lived happily ever after.

How to Tell This Story

This brief story can be made more lively by giving exotic descriptions of the castle, scary descriptions of the well, or creepy descriptions of the frog. You can modernize the story by changing the golden ball into a Gameboy or your own child's particular favorite toy. The princess could have to share playing time with the frog instead of sharing her plate with him. This is a particularly good story to tell if your child has just lost a favorite toy, or if your children don't yet understand the concept of sharing and keeping promises—the details can be easily altered to fit the particular situation.

The story emphasizes that looks aren't important.

The Giant with the Three Golden Hairs

Summary

An evil king plotted to kill a poor but lucky boy, for it was foretold that the boy would marry the king's daughter. The boy's luck saved him, but the king made him bring back three golden hairs from a giant before he let the boy alone. The lucky boy accomplished the feat, and caught the evil, greedy king in a curse at the same time.

The Characters

The lucky child: Destined to marry the princess.
The princess: Nothing special, and not a big part of the tale.
The king: An evil schemer.
An old woman: Oversaw the robber's den.
A group of robbers and their captain: Took pity on the boy and changed his fate.
Two townsmen: Each asked questions of the lucky child.
A ferryman: Sought help from the lucky child to release him from his rowing task.
The giant with golden hair: Fearsome but knowledgeable.
The giant's grandmother: Took pity on the boy and helped him.

The Plot

A child was born to a poor family. He had a star-shaped birthmark, and so was pronounced lucky. It was also prophesied that he would marry the king's daughter when he turned fourteen. The king heard about this boy and the prophecy, and so, being evil and snobbish, went to the family and paid them gold for the child. He then took the infant, placed him in a box, and threw him into a deep river, hoping to drown him. But unbeknownst to the king, the box floated off and was picked up by a miller's servant, so the child was taken into the miller's household, where he grew up.

Later on, the king had to stop at the miller's for shelter during a storm. The miller told him the miraculous story of his lucky boy's rescue from the river, and the king realized that this was the lucky boy he had tried to kill. The king schemed again, telling the miller to let this boy carry a letter from himself to the queen. In the letter, the king secretly instructed the queen to kill the lucky boy who carried it. The miller agreed to let the boy go, and the boy set out.

Not long into his journey, the boy came upon a robbers' den, where an old woman warned him to leave for fear of his life. The bold but foolish boy was too exhausted to pay heed, though, and so stayed in the hut. The robbers returned and were outraged to find him there, but the old woman explained that he bore a message to the queen. The robbers read the murderous dispatch and felt such pity for the boy that they tore it up and rewrote it to instruct the queen to have the princess and the boy married immediately.

The boy woke, took his message directly to the queen, and was immediately married to the princess. The irate king returned, and devised another scheme to doom the lucky boy. He required the boy to return with three golden hairs from the giant of the kingdom in order to keep his bride. The boy could not refuse, so he set out in search of the giant. The boy knew much about magic and magic places.

He came to a townsman, who asked him what he knew, to which the boy replied, "I know everything." The townsman thus asked him to explain why the town's fountain no longer gave any wine or water. (It was a magic fountain.) The boy answered that he would tell him when he returned from his journey, and continued on.

At the next stop another townsman asked the boy what he

knew, and the boy replied the same. The townsman then asked the boy why the town's apple tree no longer bore its golden fruit. The boy again answered that he would tell him when he returned, and continued on.

The boy next came to a ferryman on a lake, who asked the boy what he knew, and got the same reply. The ferryman asked the boy why he had to row back and forth and could never be set free. The boy gave the same answer as he had given to the two townsmen, and continued on to the giant's castle.

At the castle, the lucky boy met the giant's kind grandmother. She agreed to help him, and changed him into an ant so that the giant would not capture and eat him. She said to pay attention to what was said when she plucked out the golden hairs, and the boy would have the answers to give to the ferryman and the two townsmen.

The giant returned home and immediately smelled the boy, but the grandmother convinced him it was his imagination, and the giant settled down to have his hair combed. He soon fell asleep, but woke with a start when his grandmother plucked out a hair. The grandmother claimed that she seized hold of his hair because of a dream in which a market fountain was all dried up. The giant told her that the fountain would flow with wine again if the townspeople killed the toad that sat under a stone in the spring. He then went back to sleep.

Again the grandmother plucked a hair, and claimed it was because of a dream. This one was about the apple tree. The giant told her that the tree would bear fruit again if the townspeople killed the mouse that was gnawing at its roots. He then went back to sleep.

One more time the grandmother plucked a hair, and claimed it was because of a dream of a ferryman unable to break free of his charge. The giant told her that the ferryman only had to give the oars to the person who asked for passage to be free of his chore. The giant then went back to sleep.

After the giant left the next morning, the grandmother turned the ant back into a boy and bade him good luck. On his return, the boy crossed the lake, then told the ferryman how to break free of his curse. Then he continued to the town with the apple tree and told the townsman how to make the tree bear fruit again. His solution worked, and the townspeople rewarded him with gold. The boy then continued to the first town and told the townsman there how to restart the fountain, for which he was also rewarded in gold.

Finally, he returned to his bride and the king with the giant's hairs. The king was so impressed with the gold that he asked the boy where he could get some. The boy instructed him to go across the ferryman's lake to find it. Of course, when the king asked for passage, the ferryman handed him the oars. The king was thus punished for his greed and forced to row back and forth for all eternity, while the lucky boy and his wife lived happily ever after.

How to Tell This Story

This long tale can be broken up into two parts: the first part ending with the marriage, and the second part involving the giant and his hairs. If you only have time for a short tale, use the first section as a stand-alone story, elaborating on the journey of the infant down the river in the box, or on the robbers' den. Describe the huge wedding feast in great detail. The boy could win the king over and make the prophecy come true; the king could decide to retire and hand power over to the boy.

If you want to tell the whole story, you may not have time for lots of details, so make them memorable. Describe the fountain, the apple tree, and the ferryboat with sounds and colors that your child will remember.

The Gift of the Magi

Summary

This O. Henry story is about love and giving. A husband, Jim, and wife, Della, who loved each other very much, wanted to get each other a special Christmas present. But neither had money to spend. Della wanted to get Jim a chain for his special gold watch; Jim wanted to get Della a beautiful set of combs for her fabulous long hair. To pay for the watch chain, Della sold her hair; to pay for the combs, Jim sold his watch.

The Characters

Della: A young woman with beautiful blond (or golden) hair. She worked to save money, but was sad that things just cost too much. Otherwise she was content.

Jim: He worked hard, but just didn't earn as much money as he wished. Otherwise he was content.

The Plot

On the day before Christmas, Della knew that she had only $1.87 with which to buy her husband a Christmas present. She had wanted to get him a fob—a chain—for the gold pocket watch that had been his grandfather's, and that Jim treasured.

On the day before Christmas, Jim knew that on a salary of $20 per week (it had been $30), he couldn't afford to buy Della the Christmas present he knew she wanted most: a beautiful set of combs she had admired though a storefront window.

The only thing Della could think to do was sell her hair, which she did, for $20. With that money she bought the watch chain—it cost $21.

When Jim arrived home from work, Della told Jim what

she had done to buy his Christmas present. She was worried that Jim would be angry at her for cutting off her beautiful hair, but when she told Jim, he wasn't mad at all, and said that he loved her no matter what.

But Jim was stunned, because he had sold his gold watch to buy Della the combs.

They had sacrificed their greatest treasures to give each other the best possible Christmas present. The sacrifice each made showed the other how much love there was.

How to Tell This Story

While it's a Christmas story, you can tell it as an anniversary story, a wedding story, a Chanukah story—anything you like.

The Gingerbread Man

Summary

A fox ate a smart cookie. When a Gingerbread Man jumped out of the oven and ran away, all sorts of people and animals gave chase. He boasted of his escape to everyone he met. When the Gingerbread Man wanted to cross a stream, he accepted help from a fox, who ate him.

The Characters

The Gingerbread Man: Boastful and fast, he could outrun everyone.

The chasers: The wife who baked the Gingerbread Man, her husband, a cow, a horse, threshers, and mowers.

A fox: He knew a better way to catch the cookie.

The Plot

The farmer's wife was baking some gingerbread men when one leaped from the cookie tray when she opened the door and shouted,

"Catch me! Catch me! If you can!
Catch me! I'm the Gingerbread Man!"

She gave chase but couldn't catch the rascal. She enjoined her husband to help catch the quick cookie. He yelled, "Stop, little Gingerbread Man! I want to eat you!"

Both husband and wife couldn't catch the Gingerbread Man. A cow, then a horse, then some mowers from the field, and finally some threshers joined the chase. They couldn't catch him. Finally the Gingerbread Man met up with a fox, who said he didn't want to catch the Gingerbread Man but to help him. He offered to help the Gingerbread Man cross a stream and told the cookie to jump on his tail.

As they got farther into the stream, the fox told the Gingerbread Man the water was getting deeper and he should jump onto the fox's back. Then his shoulder. And finally in midstream, his nose. Then the fox tossed his head and gulped down the Gingerbread Man.

How to Tell This Story

When you tell this story, repeat the lines of the chasers and the Gingerbread Man each time a new character comes into the story. Soon enough you can sit quietly while your child shouts out the lines. You can even add your child's favorite characters to the cast of chasers.

Describe in great detail how the cookies were made and decorated. What was used for their eyes and mouths, noses, buttons, clothes, and hair? Were there gingerbread girls too? What about animals? What did they think when the Gingerbread Man jumped from the tray? Why did the Gingerbread Man make an escape?

Instead of the fox swallowing up the cookie, have him deliver it to the wife. She put the Gingerbread Man in the cookie jar, where his comrades welcomed him. They couldn't wait for the children to get home from school to eat them, because they liked nothing more than making children happy.

The Golden Goose

Summary

A boy called Simpleton was kind to a magical little gray man, who gave Simpleton a goose with golden feathers. With this goose Simpleton made a princess laugh and won the right to marry her. Yet he was put through three trials by the evil king, who wanted to spoil the marriage. Simpleton passed all three trials in turn, though, and married the princess.

The Characters

Simpleton: The youngest of three sons, Simpleton was treated badly by his whole family, even though he was good-hearted.

The little gray man: A magical forest-dweller, he changed into the thirsty man and then the hungry man.

The Goose: Had sticky golden feathers.

The landlord's three daughters, the parson, the sexton, and two boys: All got stuck to the golden goose.

The king: Evil and greedy.

The Princess: So solemn that she was promised in marriage to the person who could make her laugh.

The Plot

Simpleton's oldest brother went into the forest to cut wood and met the little gray man. When the little man asked for some of the boy's cake and wine, the boy selfishly refused. The little man cursed the brother and made him cut himself, so that he had to return home. Simpleton's other brother went into the forest to cut wood. He also treated the little gray man poorly and was likewise cursed. Finally, Simpleton was allowed to go into the forest to cut wood. When the little gray man appeared to him, kind Simpleton agreed to share his meal. For this kindness, the little gray man gave Simpleton a goose with golden feathers.

Simpleton then left the forest and went to an inn. There, the landlord's three daughters became curious about the goose's golden feathers, but when each tried to pluck one, they became stuck to the goose! Simpleton didn't notice them, however, and the next morning he walked away with the three in tow. The girls were spotted by the parson, who came up to them and tried to pull them away, but then he too became stuck. The same thing occurred to the sexton and two boys, until Simpleton had seven people trailing him, stuck to the goose and each other.

The group later reached a town and heard of a princess who was so sad that her father, the king, had promised her hand in marriage to anyone who could make her laugh. Simpleton led the group to the castle, and sure enough, the princes burst out laughing when she saw the group. But the king was a cheater and didn't want Simpleton for a son-in-law, so he made him pass three trials before letting him marry the princess.

First, he told Simpleton to find a man who could drink up a whole cellar full of wine. Simpleton sought help from the little gray man, but instead found a very thirsty man in the forest where the little gray man had been. He brought the man back to the castle, and the man drank the king's cellar dry.

Next, the king told Simpleton to find a man who could eat up the biggest loaf of bread in the kingdom. Again, Simpleton went to the little gray man for help; he found a very hungry man. The man ate up the huge loaf of bread.

Finally, the king told Simpleton to find a boat that could travel on both land and sea. This time, Simpleton found the little gray man, and the little gray man gave Simpleton the special boat in exchange for his proven generosity. Simpleton returned triumphantly to the king's castle and married the princess.

How to Tell This Story

"The Golden Goose" is an instructive story—it teaches the rewards of generosity. But it also contains many plot elements with which you can be creative. Instead of a golden goose, the little gray man can leave behind your child's favorite toy for Simpleton, or any object, just so long as it is something people would want to touch. You can easily exaggerate the curse and the predicament of those caught in it—make up funny situations and positions for people to get stuck to the party. Also exaggerate the thirsty man and the hungry man scenes—the thirsty man could drink up the cellar of wine, then drink up the moat around the castle, and all the fountains there too. The hungry man could eat up all the bread, cakes, and cookies in the kingdom, so that everyone got mad at the king.

Add detail about the special land and sea ship. This is also where you can easily modernize the story. Give the vehicle supersonic or even spacegoing features, and your children will pay closer attention.

One complaint that I have about this kind of story is that a princess's fate is decided by others. In the classic fairy tale, the princess has little or no free will. So, why not have the princess assign Simpleton his tasks? After all, she wanted to see if Simpleton was worth marrying. Or, while Simpleton was performing the king's assignments, the princess could have eloped with someone else. In that event, the king, so impressed by Simpleton, could reward him by naming him the king's most important adviser.

Goldilocks and the Three Bears

Summary

Goldilocks was a little girl who went walking in the woods alone and discovered a house owned by three bears. The bears had gone for a stroll, too (leaving their doors unlocked!), so Goldilocks entered their home and tried out their food and furnishings. While sleeping in one of the beds upstairs, she was discovered by the bears, and she ran away.

The Characters

Goldilocks: Young, adventurous; goes into people's—bears'—
houses when she shouldn't.
Papa Bear: Large patriarch of the bear family.
Mama Bear: The mother bear.
Baby Bear: The offspring of Mama and Papa.

The Plot

The three bears lived in a little house in the woods. One day Mama Bear made porridge for lunch for herself, Papa Bear, and Baby Bear. The porridge was too hot to eat, so the Bear family decided to go for a walk in the forest while it cooled.

Goldilocks, who was about eight years old, headed out of her house alone and into the woods about the same time the bears left their home. She discovered the bears' house in the woods and was curious. Inside, Goldilocks discovered three bowls of porridge on the table and realized she was hungry. She took a spoonful from Papa Bear's bowl, because it was the largest. Yow!—it was too hot! Then she tried Mama Bear's bowl. Brrr!—too cold! The bite from the last bowl was just right, and she ate it all up.

Next, Goldilocks tried out the chairs in the living room. Papa Bear's chair was too hard, and Mama Bear's chair was too soft. While Baby Bear's chair was most comfortable (remember, Goldilocks was a little girl), it couldn't support her weight—it broke. The Bears still hadn't returned, and Goldilocks, ever curious, went upstairs and discovered three beds. She tried all three (Papa Bear's was too high; Mama Bear's was too low), and settled on Baby Bear's bed—it was just right!

While Goldilocks was sleeping, the bears returned. Papa Bear said in a booming voice, "Someone has been eating my porridge!" Mama said the same thing in a medium voice. Both were upset, but became even more so when little Baby Bear said in a little voice, "Someone has been eating my porridge, and has eaten it all up!" Then they discovered that someone had been sitting in their chairs. Both Mama Bear and Papa Bear repeat their familiar refrain. Baby Bear says in his little voice, "Someone has been sitting in my chair, and now it's broken!"

The bears went upstairs and were distressed to find that their beds had been slept in. "Someone has been sleeping in my bed," Papa said, and Mama Bear said the same. Baby Bear, however, noted, "Someone's been sleeping in my bed, and *there she is!*" Goldilocks woke up just then. She ran down the stairs and out of the house.

How to Tell This Story

This is a very short story that doesn't make much sense to adults, although children love it. The best part of the story is that children will anticipate what the bears are going to say, since they know what Goldilocks has been up to. One fun tactic is to vary your voice with each bear's exclamation—a big, growling voice for Papa, a medium, feminine voice for Mama, and a cute little voice for Baby Bear.

The moral of this story isn't clear, since Goldilocks escaped unscathed, even though she ate the bears' food and broke the chair. You could say that Goldilocks' parents grounded her for trespassing and made her pay for repairing the chair out of her allowance.

One of my favorite variations is to have Goldilocks run home, climb into her bed, and go to sleep. (Sleep: the perfect ending for every fairy tale.)

Hansel and Gretel

Summary

Hansel and Gretel were two clever children of a very, poor unsuccessful woodcutter. (Modern-day woodcutters are usually very successful.) Their stepmother wanted to lose the children in the forest so that there would be enough food for the husband and herself. The children got lost and encountered a witch living in a gingerbread house. The witch tried to eat the children, but they outsmarted her.

The Characters

Hansel: A resourceful, cunning boy who loved and protected his sister.

Gretel: A little girl with her own smarts and a trust in her brother. Gretel was the real heroine in the end—a rarity for girls in traditional fairy tales.

The woodcutter: A wimp.

The stepmother: A diabolical, treacherous, selfish woman.
The witch: Lived in a house made of sweets and ate little children.

The Plot

A family of four tried to sustain themselves on a poor woodcutter's earnings. The stepmother persuaded the father to abandon his children in the woods, so the two could live without the responsibility of feeding them. The father didn't want to do this, but he was nagged into submission.

Hansel overheard the conversation and prepared for the inevitable by filling his pockets with pebbles. The next day, the parents took the children into the woods to collect wood; each got one piece of bread. The parents told Hansel and Gretel to go to sleep, then left them alone by a fire. Hansel, fortunately, had left a trail of pebbles behind him from the house.

While their eyes were shut, the children thought they heard their father banging his ax against a tree, but it was only a tree limb blowing against the tree trunk. The sound, though, made them believe that their father was around, so they ate their bread and fell asleep. The darkness frightened Gretel when she awoke. Hansel told her to wait until the moon rose so they could see the pebbles and follow them home.

The moon did rise, and the pebbles glittered a path home. The children knocked on the door of their house the next morning, and their father was overjoyed to see them. His wife scolded Hansel and Gretel for staying out in the woods. The family tried again to manage, but the cupboards were still bare. The stepmother was determined to lose the children in the woods.

Hansel and Gretel overheard their stepmother's words, and Hansel tried to slip outside for more pebbles. This time the stepmother locked the door. Hansel told Gretel not to cry, because he said somehow they would find their way home. The next morning, Hansel crumbled the bread his father gave

him and stuffed it in his pocket before they all headed into the
woods.

Hansel dallied, leaving a path of crumbs. His stepmother
told him to hurry up. This time, she lead the children deeper
into the woods. The stepmother told the children to lie down
and rest and said that she and their father would be back to
fetch them soon.

When they woke up, the sky was pitch-black, and they
were alone and frightened. Hansel told Gretel to wait for the
moonlight, and they would be safe. The moonlight came, but
the crumbs were gone—eaten by the birds! Hansel told her,
"We will get home somehow," and when morning came, they
started walking.

When they were too tired and hungry to walk any farther
(although they ate some berries), they fell asleep again. When
they awoke on the third morning, they were ravenous. They
continued to try to walk out of the woods. At noon, they saw a
bird and followed it to a little house. The house was made of
gingerbread and trimmed with raisins and nuts. The windows
were sugar candy and the roof was made of almond cake.

"Let's eat," said Hansel, and they started eating pieces of
the house. Suddenly a voice screeched from inside, "What animal's scratching at my door?"

The children answered, "It's just Hansel and Gretel."

They kept right on eating, their fear overcome by hunger.

An old woman opened the door and invited them inside to
eat and then to sleep in two beautiful beds. Ah, so wonderful,
thought Hansel and Gretel.

But the witch was only pretending to be kind, because she
really planned to fatten up the two children and eat them. She
put Hansel in a little cage and ordered Gretel to do housework. She kept feeding Hansel huge portions of roast beef and
potatoes to make him fat and juicy. Hansel tricked the witch
into thinking he was too skinny to eat by sticking a chicken
bone out when she wanted to feel his finger. The old witch was
nearly blind, and so couldn't see that it wasn't his finger. The

witch grew impatient, and she decided to eat him even if he wasn't fat yet.

She ordered Gretel to make some bread and light the fire. Gretel kneaded the dough, then the witch told her to crawl inside the oven to see if it was hot enough. Gretel knew what the witch wanted to do, so she said, "I don't know how." Exasperated, the witch said she would show Gretel. She put her head in the oven, and Gretel shoved the rest of her inside, then quickly bolted it shut. The witch screamed, but Gretel didn't open the door until she was dead.

Gretel let Hansel out of the cage. They explored the house, finding hidden jewels and pearls—much better than pebbles! When they arrived home, the children found their father sitting sad and alone. He gave them a hug and said that he hadn't had a happy moment since he abandoned them, and that his wife had died. Gretel showed him the jewels, and they knew their troubles were over.

How to Tell This Story

Again, we have the classic Grimm mean stepmother. The women always seem to be the mean characters in the Grimm brothers' tales. Go ahead and update such stories by changing witches to warlocks or evil forest monsters; or make mean stepmothers into hateful half-uncles or heartless supervisors. You do not have to stick to the story line. You can say that the father wanted the children out, and the stepmother went to the witch's house and saved the children. The woodcutter could be a stockbroker, down on his luck; the wife could be a nasty nanny he unwittingly hired and respected. Tell it so it works for your family, any way you like.

The gingerbread house is worth a description, and maybe you can make one with your children that day. This story lets the children be brave and clever.

A simple change that will make the story more palatable for tiny tots is to have Gretel lock the witch in a closet instead of killing her. Gretel and Hansel escaped, then Gretel told the police where to find the witch to arrest her. Gretel received a medal.

For a large change, eliminate all the gory, scary stuff and make the gingerbread house a place Hansel and Gretel were taken to because they were good or had eaten their dinners.

Jack and the Beanstalk

Summary

A boy named Jack sold his mother's only possession, a cow, at the market. He was gypped, or so his mother believed, because he sold the cow for five so-called magical beans. The man with the beans told Jack that if he planted them they'd grow to the sky by morning. Well, indeed a giant beanstalk grew, which Jack climbed. At the top he found a woman who warned Jack that her husband ate boys, but also revealed the secret of the giant's castle: Once upon a time it had belonged to Jack's father. A strange, magical lady told Jack he had to perform certain tasks to regain the castle. The next time up the stalk, Jack stole a hen that laid golden eggs. The third time, Jack stole a golden harp and was almost caught. He climbed down the beanstalk and chopped the whole thing down, killing the giant, who was trying to climb down.

The Characters

Jack: A poor boy, but he wasn't always like that. He was gullible, but his gullibility paid off. (He can also be lazy and not too careful.) Jack wanted to please his mother. By accident Jack became a hero, but maybe that was his nature, anyway.

Jack's mother: She had a sharp tongue. Didn't treat Jack all that well, but didn't mistreat him, either.

The man in the market: A mystery. Obviously he had a streak of kindness, since he was willing to do Jack good, but his motives were unclear. Deserving of more examination.

The giant's wife: A giant herself. She was a magic witch who wanted to make things right again. She didn't like the giant, and didn't like cleaning, cooking, slaving after him all the time.

The giant: An ogre, mean and ugly. He had taken possession of the castle by force. Nobody liked him, but everybody feared him.

The Plot

Jack's mother gave Jack the cow, their only possession, to sell at the market because the cow was no longer making milk. He sold the cow to a man in exchange for magic beans that the man told him would grow to the sky. Jack's mother scolded him for being conned. "You fool," she screamed at Jack.

Jack planted the beans anyway. By morning a tall beanstalk had grown to the clouds. Jack climbed the beanstalk, where he found a giant woman living in a castle. Jack asked for some food, to which the woman replied that it was Jack who would be lunch if he didn't leave immediately. "My husband," she said, "likes to eat English boys." She also explained the origin of the castle. It had belonged to an Englishman and his family, who had many magical and valuable treasures. A giant killed the Englishman and stole his treasures, but the wife and baby escaped. The mother and her child went to live with the child's nurse. The woman told Jack that he was that child. She said that in order to regain his castle, Jack had to steal a bag of gold coins, the goose that laid golden eggs, and a singing harp.

Jack pleaded for food, and she gave him some bread and cheese.

Suddenly, the giant came home. He was singing:

> *"Fee fi fo fum,*
> *I smell the blood of an Englishman.*
> *If he's alive*
> *I'll use his bones to grind my bread."*

The wife told Jack to hide in the closet. The giant insisted to his wife that he smelled an Englishman; his wife said, "You must be dreaming."

Jack waited for the giant to fall asleep while counting gold coins. Jack took a bag of the giant's coins and climbed down the beanstalk. When he got down, Jack told his mother the whole story.

After their gold ran out, Jack climbed the beanstalk again. He visited the same woman, and while he was there, the giant approached. Jack hid in the oven.

On his way out, Jack stole the goose that laid the golden eggs. He and his mother were very well off.

Jack climbed the beanstalk one more time. "Fee fi fo fum . . ." the giant chanted. His wife told him that he didn't smell an Englishman; it was a flock of sheep instead.

Later the giant fell asleep to the music of his singing, golden harp. When the giant was asleep, Jack emerged from hiding and stole the harp, which cried, "Master, master!"

Quickly, Jack climbed down the beanstalk. The giant followed Jack down, but Jack was faster. When he got to the bottom, Jack chopped the beanstalk down, and the giant fell to the ground, dead.

How to Tell This Story

You can make the giant into a monster, or make the giant into a more sympathetic character. Whatever you do, children are interested in the bigness of the giant—how big his clothes were, his shoes, his furniture, his food. You could, in fact, turn the entire story into a tale about the bigness of the giant's domain, if you wanted. The goose and magical harp are especially interesting to children; indeed, you can create brand-new stories out of these creatures. You can also create magical powers for the goose and the harp: The harp could sing to warn Jack that the giant is coming; the goose could also aid in his escape.

John Henry

Summary

John Henry was a "steel-driving man"; that's what he wanted his gravestone to read. He was born with a hammer in his hand. Much of John Henry's life was spent searching for the career that suited him best. John Henry was strong—probably the strongest man alive—but how should he use that strength, that was the question. Finally he got a job hammering spikes to make the great railroads. One day, a steam drill was introduced, and in a competition between John Henry and the drill, John Henry won. But he worked so hard that he worked himself to death.

The Characters

John Henry: Born with a hammer in his hand. Stronger than any other man. Kind, and gentle, too. Until he found his goal in life, hammering spikes into the railroad tracks, he was not fully happy.

John Henry's mother and father: Kind, too. Though supportive of John Henry's quest, they still wanted him to fulfill his household chores.

John Henry's supervisors: Appreciative of his strength. They all treated him well.

The railroad bosses: Also appreciative of John Henry's strength; still, that didn't stop them from introducing the steam drill.

The Plot

John Henry was born with a hammer in his hand and was the strongest baby anybody had ever seen. While he wielded his hammer well, his parents told him that he would have to tend to chores like picking cotton and hoeing corn. But John Henry told his mother, "Ma, I know this hammer is going to be the death of me one day."

John Henry grew up as all boys do. So one day he told his parents that picking cotton and hoeing corn didn't seem natural to him. John Henry said, "I have to find a job where I got a hammer in my hand." His parents wished him well.

The first job John Henry got was picking cotton, though that wasn't his first choice. And John Henry picked cotton and hoed corn better and faster than anybody else could—but after a while he needed to move on to a job where he could use his hammer. He never minded hard work, but it was his hammer that was his calling.

The next job John Henry got was working on a steamboat, the *Diamond Joe*, loading cargo and shoveling coal into the engine's furnace. John Henry was faster and better than anybody who had ever had that job. He looked strong, too!

One day while sailing down the Mississippi the *Diamond Joe* became stuck in mud. The boat started to sink; John Henry offered to push the *Diamond Joe* to safety. And he did.

The *Diamond Joe* went to port for repairs. In the meanwhile, John Henry was wading along the shore of the Mississippi. He saw some men laying railroad tracks and knew that was the job for him. When he asked if he could get that job, the foreman asked John Henry whether he'd laid tracks before. Although John Henry had not, he said, "I was born with a hammer in my hand." Nobody had seen anyone hammer steel as fast as John Henry. He was the best.

Soon after John Henry got the railroad job, he married a woman named Polly Ann. They loved each other very much.

After a little time the railroad offered John Henry a job

hammering the track through the Big Bend Mountain in West Virginia. This was going to be the longest railroad tunnel in America. John Henry worked harder and faster than any other man.

One day there was a cave-in. Men were trapped, and the fuse of a load of dynamite was quickly burning down to its end. John Henry threw his hammer and snuffed out the fuse.

One day a man from the railroad company brought a steam drill to the crew. The foreman said that he didn't need any new contraption—he had John Henry. "There ain't no machine faster than John Henry," the foreman said. The railroad boss challenged John Henry to a race with the machine. John Henry won that race, hammering faster and harder than he ever had—than any other man ever could. With a twenty-pound hammer in each hand, he swung so fast that his arms were a blur. At the end, though, John Henry had worked himself so hard that he just died. But he died happy, doing what he always wanted to do.

How to Tell This Story

Any story involving death requires tact and perhaps a little caution. You can always end the story with John Henry just winning; fine enough for most children. If you end the story slightly prematurely, then you might want to include a lesson: People are better than machines, or hard work beats relying on a machine.

In any event, the story of John Henry allows you the opportunity to weave in a little American history. If your child enjoys playing with trains, this is a marvelous opportunity to take advantage of that interest.

Johnny and the Three Goats

Summary

Johnny was a goatherd. One day while taking his three goats home, he walked by a turnip field with a fence that had a hole. The goats ran inside and ate the turnips. Johnny couldn't get them to leave. Neither could a fox or a rabbit. Finally a bee drove the goats out.

The Characters

Johnny: A good goatherd, but apparently not good enough.
The goats: They take advantage of an opportunity like a field of turnips.
The fox: Confident, but insecure.
The rabbit: Also confident; also insecure.
The bee: Also confident—and successful.

The Plot

Every day, Johnny took his three goats to pasture and then back home. But one day, while returning by a neighbor's field, Johnny—and the goats—saw an opening in the fence that led to a neighbor's turnip field.

How could the goats resist? Johnny knew that was wrong, and with his stick, he tried to shoo the goats out. But they were naughty and stayed. The goats just ran around and nibbled on the turnips.

Johnny sat down and cried.

Along came a fox, who asked Johnny why he was crying. The fox told Johnny not to worry; he would chase them from the field. After a while, the fox got out of breath, stopped chasing, and sat down next to Johnny and cried.

Soon a rabbit came by. He, too, said that he could chase the goats out of the field. But the rabbit also failed; then he sat down next to Johnny and the fox and cried.

Finally a bee flew by and offered to help. Johnny, the fox, and the rabbit all laughed at the bee—after all, it was so tiny. But the bee just buzzed in the ear of the largest goat. Then the bee buzzed in the goat's other ear. A loud buzzing! The goat thought the field was full of bees, and left through the hole in the fence. The bee then buzzed the other two goats, who followed the big goat out.

Johnny, the fox, and the rabbit all thanked the little bee.

How to Tell This Story

"How come the bee got the goats out?" Something like that is what your child is probably going to ask. Good question, because it provides an opportunity to tell the story's moral, which is: Don't confuse somebody's size with his or her strength.

To prolong the story—my daughter, Karen would insist on this—add more animals who fail. Add a horse, a dog, a donkey, a goose—anything and everything else.

Goats eat everything—so the myth goes—so once they've finished chomping on the turnips, they might nibble on some other plants, or even start eating the fence! There are plenty of directions in which this story can go.

Johnny Appleseed

Summary

This is the story of Johnny Appleseed and how apple trees spread around the country. Johnny Appleseed's mission in life was to ensure that this newly created country, America, was filled with apple trees. And so Johnny Appleseed carried seeds with him around the country, until he died. People across the country were grateful to him.

The Characters

Johnny Appleseed: An odd-looking but well-liked man. He wore a piece of rope as a belt and an old shirt. There was only one thing he ever wanted to do—grow apple trees.

The angel: This character told Johnny Appleseed to start his quest.

People: Everyone is friendly to Johnny Appleseed.

Animals: Animals like Johnny Appleseed too.

The Plot

Johnny Appleseed was an odd, eccentric man. He had a scraggly beard, rarely wore shoes, sometimes didn't wear a belt. He was once called by another name, Johnny Chapman, but most everybody, including Johnny Appleseed, had forgotten that name. "Johnny Appleseed," one farmer joked: "That's what you should be called."

Johnny Appleseed was born in Massachusetts just before the American Revolution. Massachusetts was a beautiful farm state, with rolling hills and apple orchards everywhere. Johnny worked in an apple orchard as a child and saw apples everywhere.

After the Revolution, people moved across the country into places where there had been no people, and there were no apples. Johnny wondered where people would get their apples, and one night he dreamed an angel told him to go on a journey planting apple seeds.

And that's what Johnny Appleseed did. Once he found a pot and used that as a hat to keep the rain off his head, which made him look even odder. But that wasn't important, because during the years that Johnny Appleseed roamed the country, people came to know him and love him. When Johnny Appleseed's boots wore out, he didn't even bother to replace them; he just continued on his way planting apple seeds. But, miraculously, his feet never hurt him; not when walking on snow, not when walking through the mountains.

He was never bothered by wild animals, either. One day Johnny Appleseed came upon a wolf that had been caught in a trap. Johnny Appleseed rescued the wolf, which then followed Johnny Appleseed along, just like a puppy dog. Although settlers usually killed wolves, they left Johnny Appleseed's wolf alone.

Once every couple of years Johnny Appleseed would return east for more apple seeds.

Then one day Johnny Appleseed got caught in a fierce storm. He made his way to a cabin, but the cabin was locked. So Johnny Appleseed lay down on the front porch and went to sleep. He didn't feel the cold. There he had a dream. And in his dream, the angel returned and told Johnny Appleseed that his work was completed and he could now rest. He passed away with a smile on his face.

How to Tell This Story

You can skip the angel or even the dream about the angel. It's absolutely fine (possibly even better) for Johnny Appleseed to have simply decided to start this mission on his own, without the dream.

The story is pretty short, but there's ample opportunity to teach about American history through Johnny Appleseed. The problems faced by the settlers, the conflicts between the settlers and the Indians, the places the settlers visited, the origins of colonies and states, the purpose behind the Revolution—these are all things that you can talk about while telling the story of Johnny Appleseed. Indeed, children learn faster—and remember more—through stories than through any other means.

The Lion and the Mouse

Summary

A lion decided not to eat a mouse that woke the lion up because the mouse promised to help the lion someday in the future. Some time later the mouse rescued the lion from a hunter's net.

The Characters

The lion: Fearless—a regular lion.
The mouse: Smart.

The Plot

Once upon a time a mouse ran across the paw of a sleeping lion. The lion got mad because the mouse had waked him up, and he said to the mouse, "I'm going to eat you up."

The mouse said, "Please, Mr. Lion, don't eat me. I promise that someday I will help you!"

The lion said that there was nothing a mouse could do for a lion, and he laughed at the very idea, but he let the mouse go anyway.

A week later the lion was trapped by a net some hunters had left as a wild animal trap. The mouse found the lion and chewed a hole big enough in the net for the lion to escape.

How to Tell This Story

I view this as a cautionary tale about waking somebody (say, your parents on a Sunday morning). But it's mostly a fun story about the relationship between strength and ability. To emphasize that, after the lion is captured, show how he roars, struggles, and claws at the net—but nothing happens.

After the mouse let the lion out, they obviously became best friends, and did everything together. This story can be the springboard to a whole set of tales about the lion and the mouse.

Other details: Have the mouse talk in a squeaky mouse voice and the lion in a deep growling voice.

You can also talk about the people who set the trap. Maybe they weren't hunters; they were zookeepers or circus owners trying to capture animals. The lion told the mouse that he was scared to be taken away to the zoo or made to jump through flaming hoops in the circus. Give the lion motivation to want to escape; give some passion to his pleading with the mouse to help him get free.

The Little Match Girl

Summary

This is a sad story, but even sad stories have their place. It's about a poor little girl who froze to death one winter night. But before she died, she had the most wonderful visions—visions of a beautiful house, visions of her deceased grandmother. She saw these things when she struck her matches that she was supposed to sell.

The Characters

The little match girl: She was so poor she had to sell matches. She was always cold and hungry. You get the impression that she was happier dead than alive.

The little match girl's father: He never makes an appearance in the story, but was clearly mean to the little match girl. He beat her, and only saw her as a way of earning money.

The grandmother: The little match girl loved her grandmother, and her grandmother loved the little match girl. In the story she is already dead.

The Plot

The last night of the year was cold, and there was stiff, chilly wind. A little girl wandered the streets without a coat, shoes, hat, or gloves. She had been wearing slippers, but they fell off, and before she could get to them, a boy grabbed them and ran away.

The little girl carried many matches in her pockets. She had to sell the matches or her father would beat her.

For warmth, the girl huddled between two houses. She was so cold that she struck a match for warmth. As she peered into the match, she saw a room with a blazing fireplace, and a beautiful brass pot in the fireplace. It was so real that it felt warm. But when the match burned down, singeing her fingers, the room vanished.

She lit another match. Now she could see a room with a table set for a feast. There was a goose stuffed with apples and pears on the table; the goose leaped down from the table and walked over to her. But before the goose reached the little girl, the match went out.

The little girl lit another match. Now she was under a Christmas tree, the most beautiful and best-decorated tree she could imagine. When she went to touch the tree, the flame on her match died.

But the lights of the tree didn't seem to go out. She looked up and realized that it wasn't the light of the tree that she was seeing—it was the stars. Then she saw a shooting star and thought, "Oh, somebody must have died." The little girl's grandmother, who was the only person who had ever loved the little girl, had told her that whenever a shooting star falls, it means that somebody has died.

The little match girl lit another match. When she did, her grandmother appeared in the middle of a bright light. "Grandmother! I've missed you so much. Please take me with you. I know that when the match blows out you'll disappear like the pot and the goose and the Christmas tree."

The little girl lit all the rest of her matches, because she wanted her grandmother to stay. Her grandmother held the little match girl, and she didn't feel cold or hungry or uncomfortable any more. Together they walked to heaven.

The next day people found the little match girl dead against a stone wall. She looked pale, but there was a smile on her face. People were sad, because the little girl held all these burned matches in her hand, and they thought she must have been trying to warm herself. Only the little match girl knew that she had started the New Year so happy.

How to Tell This Story

If you're telling your child "The Little Match Girl," it's for a special reason. There's nothing I need to say about how to tell this story.

Of course, with not too much modification, you can eliminate the part about the match girl dying. Perhaps she got invited inside for a warm meal!

Little Red Riding Hood

Summary

This is a story of well-intentioned girl, called Little Red Riding Hood because she always wore a red cape. Her mother sent her off to her grandmother's house, warning Red not to stop or leave the path. She was detoured by a clever wolf who plotted to eat her and her grandmother. Both were gobbled up. A hunter passing by looked in on the grandmother and found the wolf. He opened the wolf's stomach with a knife and released the grandmother and girl. Both were fine, and Red learned an important lesson.

The Characters

Little Red Riding Hood: A beloved, adorable little girl who always wore her favorite red cape and hood.

Her mother: She gave her daughter good advice and trusted her to deliver food to the girl's grandmother.

The wolf: A wicked, clever, hungry, talking wolf.

The grandmother: Weak and bedridden. She doted on her granddaughter and had made her the red cape.

The hunter: He was searching for this wolf but was smart enough not to shoot but to carve instead. He knew the grandmother and occasionally looked in on her.

The Plot

Little Red Riding Hood was the nickname of a pretty and sweet little girl whose favorite coat was a red cape and hood her grandmother had made.

Her mother sent her out with a basket of sandwiches and

cookies for her sick grandmother, reminding her to go quickly, since her grandmother was ill. Little Red Riding Hood promised to stay on the path. She met a wolf. Red didn't know to fear the wolf and explained to him that she was in a hurry to see her grandmother on the other side of the woods. The hungry wolf pointed out how beautiful the forest was and suggested she slow down and look around. Red decided to pick some flowers for her grandmother along the way.

Meanwhile, the wolf went to the grandmother's house, posing as Little Red Riding Hood. The Grandmother had left the door open (the Bear family in "Goldilocks" did this, too—best to lock your doors!). The wolf came in and ate her up. Then he slipped under the bedcovers dressed in her gown and nightcap.

When Red Riding Hood arrived at her grandmother's, something didn't look right about her grandmother. Red exclaimed:

"Grandmother, what big ears you have!"

The wolf answered, "The better to hear you with, my dear."

"Grandmother, what big eyes you have!" Red Riding Hood said.

"The better to see you with, my dear," came the reply.

"Grandmother, what big hands you have!"

"The better to hug you with, my dear."

Last comment: "Grandmother, what big teeth you have!"

The wolf answered, "The better to eat you with!" and promptly gobbled her up.

The wolf was so full he couldn't walk; he just lay back down in the bed.

A hunter, a friend of the grandmother's, was passing by the grandmother's house and saw the door open. He was worried about the old lady and went inside. He found the wolf asleep and was about to shoot his nemesis, when he realized the grandmother was no where to be seen. Instead, he cut open the wolf's stomach, and out popped Red. Red thanked the hunter profusely, saying how dark and scary it was in there. Then the grandmother came out, too, and the hunter replaced them with rocks inside the wolf's stomach.

The wolf woke up and tried to run away. The rocks were too heavy, and he fell down dead. Red, the grandmother, and the brave hunter sat down and shared the basket of goodies. Red learned never to stray from the path or talk to strangers again.

How to Tell This Story

This story will help you emphasize the importance of never talking with strangers and of going where you're supposed to go.

Some dialogue can be added between the mother and Red, between the wolf and Red, and between the hunter and Red. You might want to describe the forest, the path, and other animals she saw on her way.

Make the story longer by telling how many coats Red tried until her grandmother made her the red one that gave Red her name. Maybe your child has a nickname too with a story behind it?

Shorten the story by beginning with Red already on the path in her red cape. However, do not leave out the part where Red noticed how strange her grandmother looked. Most children love this part, and they remember the questions and answers.

You can replace the hunter with a woodcutter to reduce the atmosphere for violence.

Want to avoid bloodshed entirely in this story? Then the wolf didn't eat the grandmother; he just locked her in the closet, hoping to fool Red into giving him the basket of goodies.

When he told Red, "The better to eat you with, my dear," he leaped out of the bed and tried to grab her, but Red was a fast runner. She escaped into the forest, where she found her

friend the woodcutter. He ran back to the house with his ax
and scared the wolf off into the forest. Grandma, Red, and the
woodcutter all ate the goodies, then lay down and went nighty-
night, knowing the scared wolf would never return!

The Magic Pot

Summary

A poor Korean farmer came across a brass pot while
digging in his small vegetable garden. The pot, the farmer and
his wife discovered, made two of anything you put inside it.
First they tried odds and ends; then money. By accident, the
farmer's wife fell into the pot—and there were now two of
her! An odd marriage. But accidents can happen again, and
the farmer leaped—or fell?—into the pot, which solved their
problem.

The Characters

Mr. Kim-Soon: A poor farmer.
Mrs. Kim-Soon: The poor farmer's wife.

The Plot

Mr. and Mrs. Kim-Soon lived in a tiny cottage on the side
of a mountain. They had a small patch of land on which to grow
food.

One day Mr. Kim-Soon unearthed a large brass pot, which
was itself unusual, because the farmer thought he knew every
inch of that soil. Too big for a cooking pot, too small for a bath,
Mrs. Kim-Soon decided.

Then she dropped a hairpin into the pot. When she reached

inside to retrieve the pin, there were two identical pins. After checking to see that no hairpins were missing, Mr. and Mrs. Kim-Soon experimented by putting in a sack of lentils. Out came two sacks! Then they tried their purses; out came two purses.

Mr. and Mrs. Kim-Soon put in purse after purse until they decided just putting in money would be simpler.

That evening Mrs. Kim-Soon put in some rice and out came enough rice for an entire meal. She turned their one candle into twenty.

Mr. and Mrs. Kim-Soon would never be wanting again.

The next day, Mrs. Kim-Soon was making more cabbage in the magic brass pot when Mr. Kim-Soon walked in the door. She balanced the bundles of cabbage while running over to greet her husband, but lost her balance and fell into the pot. Mr. Kim-Soon pulled Mrs. Kim-Soon out by her legs, but out of the pot emerged two Mrs. Kim-Soons, exactly alike. Mrs. Kim-Soon exclaimed that she would not put up with another Mrs. Kim-Soon in the house.

Mrs. Kim-Soon said, "Put her back in the pot," but Mr. Kim-Soon was quick to point out that that would only make more Mrs. Kim-Soons. Mr. Kim-Soon took a few steps backward and fell—was it an accident?—into the pot.

Mrs. Kim-Soon pulled him out. Then she pulled out the other Mr. Kim-Soon.

Now there wasn't a problem of what to do with the extra Mrs. Kim-Soon.

The two new Mr. and Mrs. Kim-Soons set up house next door. Their neighbors thought it was curious that Mr. and Mrs. Kim-Soon suddenly prospered, and that a couple who looked a lot like Mr. and Mrs. Kim-Soon had moved in next door. A close relation of Mr. and Mrs. Kim-Soon said that it was evident that Mr. and Mrs. Kim-Soon had become so rich that they had decided to have two of everything, including themselves.

How to Tell This Story

As you can imagine, in the beginning, Mr. and Mrs. Kim-Soon did not eat meat often; when they had excess food (which was not often), they traded it for necessities such as oil for their lamps, and clothing. They lived in a kind of old-world, small-village poverty. Yet they were happy.

But they were much happier after they found the brass pot. Invent some dialogue by imagining you had found such a pot. Now imagine that suddenly you had two of the same wife—or husband. There would be a bit of confusion, to say the least. The bantering between Mr. and Mrs. Kim-Soon must have been amusing.

You can spend some time describing their house, their clothing, and, of course, the big brass pot.

There's no end to what can happen: The couples could have twins by putting their child in the pot. What about quadruplets?

The Mouse's Wedding

Summary

A magician and his wife enchanted a mouse and turned it into a little girl so they could raise her as their own child. When it came time for her to marry, no suitable groom could be found until a mouse was offered. However, they had to return her to her original form so she could marry a mouse.

The Characters

The magician: He seized the opportunity to have a family, and he gave his daughter what she really wanted.

The magician's wife: She wanted her child to be happy.

The mouse: She knew what she wanted to be when she grew up.

The Plot

As a gypsy magician was bathing in the river, a passing hawk accidentally dropped a mouse from his beak, and it landed right under the magician's nose. He closed his eyes and opened them, and the mouse was still there. So he took the mouse and turned her into a fine little girl, because he and his wife were childless. His wife was very happy and vowed to raise the girl properly.

The years passed quickly, and soon it was time for the little girl to marry. The magician and his wife began discussing suitable husbands with their daughter. The sun? The daughter said the sun was too hot and his rays would burn her skin. The sun recommended the cloud as a suitable partner, because he was stronger and more powerful. But the daughter refused, because the cloud was too scary, and besides, he hid everything, making it seem dirty. The cloud thought the wind would be a good match, because he was even stronger than the cloud. The daughter refused, because the wind was too cold and changeable. The wind said the mountain was more powerful, because the wind couldn't move the mountain. The girl said no to the mountain as well, because it was too tough. The mountain said the mouse was more powerful than he was, because a mouse tunneled in him and made him crumble. The mouse suited the girl exactly. So the magician changed the girl back into a mouse, and she married her mouse love.

How to Tell This Story

This story can go on endlessly when you ask your child to suggest suitable husbands for the mouse-girl. The suggestions will probably be silly, but they'll delight your child. Try using this story on long car trips and you'll get about an hour without hearing "Are we there yet?"

Try imagining silly situations for the magician and his wife with their daughter and son-in-law. What happened when the family gathered for Thanksgiving? Where did the mice sit? Did they frighten their relatives? What did they eat? What happened when the grandparents baby-sat the mouse children? Did the mice live in a dollhouse in the magician's house?

The Mouse, The Bird, and the Sausage

Summary

There once was a mouse and a bird and a sausage who lived together. They each had their own duties to perform to keep their household running smoothly. Unfortunately, the bird was convinced by another bird that he had been doing the brunt of the work, so the three switched duties to demonstrate that all was fair. Each of these rotated duties was so ill suited to the mouse, bird, and sausage, though, that they each perished in performing them.

The Characters

The bird: The bird's job was to fetch wood.
The mouse: The mouse made up the fire and drew water.
The sausage: The sausage cooked the food.
Another bird: This bird made the first bird feel foolish.

The Plot

The bird, the mouse, and the sausage lived in harmony in their house, each doing a fair share of the work. The bird collected wood, the mouse made the fire and set the table, and the sausage cooked the food. One day, as the bird was flying home with the day's wood, another bird spoke to him and called him a fool, convincing him that the bird's work was really the toughest job and that the mouse and the sausage were taking advantage of him.

Feeling slighted, the bird went home and complained to the mouse and the sausage. Despite their pleas, the bird refused to carry on as before, so the mouse and the sausage had to agree to switch duties. They agreed that from then on, the sausage would fetch the wood, the mouse would cook the food, and the bird would make the fire and set the table.

On the first day trying out this arrangement, the sausage went to get the wood. He met a dog and was promptly eaten. The bird went out in search of the sausage, discovered his plight, and, saddened, returned with the wood himself. The mouse then tried to prepare the food as the sausage used to do, by sticking herself in the pot to flavor the broth, but as she was no sausage, she burned and drowned. Finally, the bird, while searching for the mouse, accidentally knocked over the woodpile, which caught fire. The bird tried to fetch water from the well to put it out, but fell in the well and drowned.

How to Tell This Story

This brief story is a good before-bed quickie for children who don't like to do their chores. Although it has a dismal ending for the bird, the mouse, and the sausage, it doesn't have the gruesomeness of some other tales. You can paint a vivid picture of each character performing his or her duties (make the characters male or female as you prefer). Act out their chores—flap your arms with the bird, blow on the fire like the mouse, and stir up the stew with the sausage. If you want to tone down the ending, you can have the sausage work out a deal with the dog to be his personal chef in exchange for not getting eaten; or maybe the mouse made a really awful stew, and perhaps the bird couldn't get the fire started. Then, for the ending, the bird could realize his folly—perhaps apologizing to the mouse and the sausage and opening up a restaurant with them.

The Owl and the Pussycat

Summary

This is a lovely poem, but it can be told as a story as well. As a story, it takes on a different tone, but is still enchanting. The Owl and the Pussycat, who are in love, went sailing. They were in search of a ring for the Pussycat. All they had was five dollars (British pounds in the original story); they bought a ring from Piggy.

The Characters

The Owl: A lovely bird, an "elegant fowl," in love with the Pussycat.

The Pussycat: "A beautiful Pussy," who loves her Owl.

Piggy-wig: Also known as Pig and Piggy. A kind pig, because he sells a ring to the Owl cheaply.

The Turkey: An animal with the power to marry other animals.

The Plot

The Owl and the Pussycat went on a boat trip. They took some supplies and a guitar, with which the Owl played a love song. After sailing for a year and a day, they arrived at the land of the Bong-trees. There in the woods they found Piggy-wig, who had a ring at the end of his nose. The Owl asked Piggy if he'd sell his ring for one shilling; Piggy agreed. The next day they got married by the Turkey, and danced a wedding dance by the light of the moon.

How to Tell This Story

If you're looking for a quickie, "The Owl and the Pussycat" is the one. Even adding certain details—the kind of boat, what the Owl and the Pussycat did for the year they were at sea—doesn't add much to the story.

But you may discover that your child wants to know "more" about the "other" animals in this story. That's fine; just add more critters. The dog can be the best man, a peacock can play the piano, a camel can give them a ride after the wedding. This is a story about an animal party. The animals are having a good time, doing what people do—that's what children like to hear.

Paul Bunyan

Summary

Paul Bunyan was the greatest lumberjack there ever was. And the biggest, too. How big? Well, it was Paul Bunyan who dug out the Mississippi River.

The Characters

Paul Bunyan: A giant lumberjack. His size didn't bother him, because it just made it easier for him to wield an ax. Paul

Bunyan wore a lumberjack's red-and-black-checked shirt and suspenders.

Paul Bunyan's mother and father: Although they loved their son, they were relieved when he stopped growing, and later relieved when he left home. (They couldn't afford to feed him!)

Other lumberjacks: They were a bit envious of Paul Bunyan because he could cut trees so fast.

Babe: The blue ox was Paul's best friend.

Sourdough Sam, the cook: He could mix and make four hundred pancakes a day!

The Plot

Paul Bunyan was born big: At birth he weighed eighty-six pounds. He was quickly on his way to becoming the best lumberjack there ever was—not to mention the biggest! He was born in Maine, or perhaps New Hampshire, or Vermont; nobody knew for certain.

When he was a baby, just rolling in his cradle, the sound would knock over trees for miles around. But because Paul was so big, his parents could hardly afford to feed him; his father had to make Paul a new pair of boots every day! When Paul stopped growing, he was as tall as the largest pine tree. (Well, maybe not really, but you know how legends are.) When Paul left home, his parents had to climb a ladder to kiss him goodbye.

Paul Bunyan came to a logging camp, where he asked for a job. With one swing of his ax, Paul felled twenty trees. He used a special ax, too. Paul couldn't stay at that logging camp, because if he kept up his work, there would be no trees left for the other loggers to cut.

One thing Paul was careful about: For every tree he cut, he planted a new one. That way he wouldn't damage the land.

The next winter was called the Winter of Blue Snows, because it was so cold that the snow looked blue—too cold for anyone to go outside, except Paul Bunyan. One day, Paul found a cold ox, a baby blue ox, in the snow. He took the ox home and named her Babe. Paul Bunyan and Babe became a team; Paul cut the trees and Babe hauled them. Paul would yell the loudest "Timber" whenever he felled a tree.

But they worked alone, because no logging company could keep Paul Bunyan fed. In just one breakfast Paul would eat four hundred pancakes, eight dozen eggs, twenty pounds of bacon, and twelve loaves of bread, and drink two gallons of orange juice and coffee. So Paul started his own logging camp on the Onion River in the North Woods of Minnesota. This was the best logging camp around: It was the biggest, and, thanks to Sourdough Sam, the chef, it had the best food anywhere. Everything was big (especially when it came to food) at Paul Bunyan's camp. They had to drain a small lake to provide space to mix pancake batter in; the griddle was so big that the cooks had to skate with shoes of bacon just to keep it greased.

Paul Bunyan's camp moved from place to place. Once there was a logging road so crooked that nobody could haul trees along it. So Paul Bunyan attached Babe to the road with rope and pulled the road straight. What a sound that made!

Paul Bunyan had many accomplishments. He invented the double-edged ax; he dug out the St. Lawrence River and straightened the Round River. He created the Mississippi because his crew needed a canal through which to move their logs. In the process, the excess rock became the Rocky and Appalachian Mountains!

After Paul Bunyan's work was done in the lower forty-eight states (though there weren't forty-eight states yet), he moved on to Alaska.

How to Tell This Story

Kids love to hear about big things, so you won't disappoint anyone by describing the giant size of everything that Paul Bunyan ate, wore, and used. Your audience will also be naturally curious about Babe—you can bet that having an ox as a pet is unusual enough to delight them.

Paul Bunyan is an American legend, and you can certainly leave it at that. Alternatively, you can use it to talk about the environment. After all, Paul felt it was important to plant a tree for every one he cut down.

The Princess and the Pea

Summary

A prince was able to find a true princess to marry with the pea test: The real princess, though haggard-looking, proved her worth by being delicate enough to detect a pea beneath twenty mattresses and twenty featherbeds.

The Characters

The prince: Fairly nondescript, he had trouble finding a real princess to marry.

The king and queen: The king found the true princess, and the queen devised the test.

The true princess: Delicate as a princess should be. (Or, if you prefer, just astute and sensitive.)

The Plot

The prince searched the world over for a real princess to marry, but couldn't find a princess without some defect. Beauty and perfection were crucial to him. He returned home, saddened. Later, during a frightful storm, a princess knocked at the castle door, begging for shelter. Soaking and disheveled, she did not appear to be a princess at all. To test her claim, the queen placed a pea under twenty mattresses and twenty featherbeds for the princess to sleep on.

The next morning, the princess complained of discomfort. The court proclaimed her a real princess, for only a real princess would be delicate enough to detect a pea under twenty mattresses and twenty featherbeds. The prince and princess married, and the pea was placed in the royal museum.

How to Tell This Story

This brief story could use elaboration. You can add a description of the twenty mattresses and featherbeds, or describe where and how badly the princess ached the following morning. And while children seem to enjoy the notion of the "pea test," they might not understand why delicate skin was at such a premium. Maybe the prince was allergic to peas and needed to marry someone who could detect them? (But he loved broccoli!) Maybe the princess found the pea, but only agreed to marry the prince if the queen and the court started eating their vegetables and stopped wasting them by sticking them under people's mattresses.

The story could also be revamped and improved from a girl's point of view in any number of ways to make the point that there are more important qualities in a princess than delicacy—like spunk and ingenuity.

Suppose the princess felt the pea and couldn't sleep, but decided, instead of complaining, to find out what was the matter. She searched through all the mattresses and featherbeds, pulled out the pea, and then slept soundly.

Now suppose she didn't sleep well because of the pea and told the prince so the next morning. When he proclaimed that she had passed the test, she told him that she didn't want to marry someone who would set up such a silly test to find a wife. She then got a job as a mattress tester.

Puss in Boots

Summary

This is a story about a very smart cat named Puss, who liked his master very much, but who also knew that the only way he could better himself was to better his master. Puss, though a number of tricks and outright cunning, not to mention proficiency at being a cat, turned his master from a poor man into the wealthiest man in the kingdom. He accomplished this by tricking the king into believing that Puss's master was a marquis, then by tricking an evil, wealthy ogre into turning into a mouse, which Puss ate.

The Characters

Puss: A smart cat who can talk. He's very good at being a cat: cunning, clever, unpredictable, and, mostly, hungry. He's certainly a lot smarter than his master, and probably smarter than anyone else in the kingdom.

Puss's master: In the 1990s he would be a servant to his cat. Come to think of it, who isn't in any century? The cat's master (whom you can give a name to if you want) was the poorest of several sons.

The king: A good ruler, and the only other thing we can really say about him is that he, too, had much faith in what cats have to say.

The princess: Beautiful, rich, and single. The king wanted her married, and Puss wanted her to marry his master.

The ogre: Rich and awful; could turn himself into any creature he wanted. The ogre became so wealthy by being a great landowner; people had to pay tribute to him to get anything.

The Plot

When a poor miller died, he left his three sons everything he had, which wasn't much. The older two sons took everything they could, leaving the youngest son with just a cat. Being poor and hungry, the son decided to eat the cat.

Puss wasn't enthusiastic about this idea. He told his master, "Give me a sack and some boots, and you'll discover that you got the best share of the estate." The son didn't believe the cat, though he respected Puss's cleverness, and so Puss went on his way.

Puss put some bran and leaves in the sack near where rabbits lived. He then stretched out looking like a dead cat. A few moments later a dumb bunny jumped into the sack; Puss closed the sack and brought the rabbit to the king.

Puss had decided to fib a little and claim that his master was called the Marquis of Carabas. Puss told the king that the marquis had instructed him to present the king with this gift, a rabbit. The king was pleased.

The next day, the cat captured some quail the same way, and presented them to the king. The king was pleased. For the next two months, Puss continued to present the king with gifts from the marquis.

But Puss had a bigger plan. On a day Puss knew that the king and his beautiful daughter would be at the river, he told his master to bathe in the river, which the marquis did without knowing why. When the king and his daughter passed by, Puss yelled, "Help! My master and lord, the Marquis of Carabas, is drowning!" The king recognized the cat and told his servants to save the marquis.

After the marquis was rescued, Puss told the king that his lord's clothes had been carried away by the river. (Puss had hidden the clothes, which were pauper's clothes.) The king gave the marquis some fine clothes to wear.

Puss's master never looked better—in fact, the king's

daughter took a liking to him. The king asked the marquis to ride in his coach.

Puss ran ahead of the coach and told all those he met that they must tell the king that all their land belonged to the Marquis of Carabas—or they would be killed. So when the king inquired who owned the land he was passing through, the people replied, "The Marquis of Carabas." The king and daughter were impressed by the amount of land under the marquis's ownership.

Finally, the coach reached the ogre's castle. In fact, it was the ogre who owned the land that the king had just driven through.

The cat had to deal with the ogre. Puss said to the ogre, "I've heard that you can change yourself into any animal."

"That's right," said the ogre. "Now watch me become a lion!" Puss shook in his boots.

Puss then said, "I've heard that you can transform yourself into any creature, no matter how small, including a mouse. But I don't believe that."

"I'll show you!" the ogre said, and he turned himself into a mouse. Whereupon the cat pounced on the mouse and ate it.

When the coach arrived, Puss said, "Welcome to the Marquis of Carabas's castle." The king was so impressed that he immediately offered the marquis his daughter's hand in marriage.

How to Tell This Story

Beware. The first time I told "Puss in Boots" to my three-year-old daughter, Karen, she immediately wanted me to tell her another Puss in Boots story. Quickly, I had to invent a sequal.

Rather than "marquis," you might want to say "earl." Small children don't know what an earl is either, but it's an easier word for them to pronounce.

The plot of "Puss in Boots" is somewhat complicated for children under five years old to follow, but that won't detract from their enjoyment. One change you might consider—and you've probably already considered it—is to lose the part about the king offering the marquis his daughter's hand. After all, daughters are not given away.

Rapunzel

Summary

Rapunzel is the story of a child who was raised by an evil witch and who grew long, beautiful hair. Rapunzel lived in a tower, and the only way up to her room was to climb her hair. Rapunzel saw nobody but the witch until a prince wandered by one day and climbed up her hair. The witch punished Rapunzel, and later the prince was hurt falling from the tower; but eventually the prince and Rapunzel lived happily ever after.

The Characters

Rapunzel's mother: Wanted a child, and after much wanting became pregnant. Strangely, she coveted a vegetable growing in the witch's garden called a rapunzel. (Is this the witch's doing?) Her need for the rapunzel was so great that she became pale and weak.

Rapunzel's father: Also wanted a child badly, and yielded to his wife's needs. They both disappear from the story shortly after Rapunzel is born.

The witch: An evil, mysterious character, with the classic, repulsive look of a witch. Her powers seemed limited only by her inclinations. Despite her evilness, there was a hint of loneliness and pity about her. Her motives were unclear. Called Mother Gothel by Rapunzel.

Rapunzel: The star of the story. It's never known how Rapunzel's hair became so long—perhaps genetic, perhaps a consequence of the witch's powers. Rapunzel was beautiful and lonely, lonelier even than the witch. How Rapunzel occupied her day isn't clear; perhaps braiding and unbraiding her hair was a full-time activity.

The prince: Handsome and valiant, like all princes. Not much substance, so the prince's character and looks can be embellished as much as you like.

The Plot

A husband and wife longed for a child, and after many years the wife became pregnant.

The couple lived in a house adjacent to a witch's house. From their house they could see the witch's garden, which was surrounded by a high wall.

The wife became enchanted, almost enthralled, with rapunzel, an unusual leafy vegetable that grew in the witch's garden; she grew pale and weak because she could not have any rapunzel. Finally the husband went into the witch's garden, gathered some rapunzel, and made a salad for them.

When the witch found out (you expected she wouldn't?), she threatened to cast a terrible spell on the husband and wife. Only by promising the witch their child could they avoid the spell.

Almost immediately afterward, Rapunzel was spirited away by the witch. When Rapunzel was twelve, she was made to live alone in a tower in the forest. Over the years, Rapunzel grew the longest, most beautiful hair in the world. Rapunzel herself became the most beautiful woman in the world. The only way up to Rapunzel's room in the tower was by climbing up her hair, which she had to braid to make this possible. That was how the witch brought food and other necessities.

"Rapunzel, Rapunzel, let down your hair, and I will climb up the golden stair" was the witch's frequent request.

One day a prince wandered by. He heard Rapunzel singing from her room and became captivated. One day he hid near the tower and watched the witch say, "Rapunzel, Rapunzel, let down your hair."

The next night he visited the tower and called, "Rapunzel, Rapunzel, let down your hair." When he got to Rapunzel's room, she was frightened, because she had never seen a man before. But the prince was kind, and Rapunzel decided she wanted to marry him. The prince visited many times more.

The witch was unaware of the prince's visits until Rapunzel asked the witch why she was so much heavier climbing up her hair than the prince. The witch was angry, cut Rapunzel's hair off, and drove her into the wilderness.

When the prince came to visit, he climbed up Rapunzel's hair, but the witch was at the other end. The prince, in grief, leaped from the tower. Not killed, he was blinded by landing on thorns.

The prince wandered the wilderness for many years. Finally he heard that familiar, sweet voice. It was Rapunzel, who hugged the prince and wept on him. Her tears restored the prince's sight. They lived happily ever after.

Alternate ending: The prince climbed up Rapunzel's hair and saw the witch at the other end. The witch tried to push him off the tower, but he pulled her by the hair out the window. She fell into the moat. The prince went off in search of Rapunzel, found her, and married her.

How to Tell This Story

Rapunzel can be shortened by skipping ahead twelve years: "Rapunzel, captured by a witch, lived in the tower of a castle" is a fair beginning.

Or you can embellish the story. The witch's castle was cold and dark. Paintings of witch ancestors covered the walls.

(Where do witches come from, anyway?) Preface the prince's appearance with some background about his character—perhaps he was an archer, perhaps a clever hunter. How did the witch raise Rapunzel? How did she dress Rapunzel?

Because the story takes place over many years, you have the opportunity to fill in those years with details. Rather than just saying, "The prince wandered the forest for years," describe how the prince lived during those years. What animals helped him? Maybe the prince and Rapunzel wandered within feet of each other. Rapunzel could have been sleeping under a bed of leaves while the prince was walking by, never noticing her.

The Red Shoes

Summary

A poor orphan girl was taken in by a wealthy, almost blind woman who unknowingly bought her fancy red (and wholly inappropriate) shoes for her confirmation. The girl could think of nothing but her red dancing shoes and was punished for her vanity—she could not take the shoes off, and they continued dancing. Exhausted, she finally begged to have her feet cut off, and when she was truly repentant, her soul went to heaven.

The Characters

The peasant girl: Her only fault was that she was struck with vanity and an attachment to her red shoes.

The old lady: A good woman who unfortunately can't see very well.

The old soldier with a crutch: The spook of the story—he encouraged the girl's vanity and haunted her.
The angel: A frightening figure who cursed the shoes.

The Plot

An orphaned peasant girl was given a home by a kindly old woman who could not see very well. The wealthy woman bought the girl new things, including a new pair of shoes. The girl picked out a fancy pair of red shoes that resembled some she had seen a princess wearing. The girl chose to wear these shoes to her confirmation because they were so charming. The shoes' redness upset everyone in the church. The blind old woman, informed that the shoes were red, warned the child not to wear them in church again.

But the girl wanted to wear the shoes for her confirmation. On the way to the church, she ran into an old soldier with a strange long red beard. The soldier slapped the soles of her shoes and exclaimed, "Such beautiful dancing shoes! They stick tight for dancing." The girl was in love with her shoes and forgot to say the Lord's Prayer at her confirmation.

As they left the church, the old soldier said again, "Such beautiful dancing shoes." The vain girl did a little dance in them, but when she tried to stop, the shoes kept on dancing. With everyone's help, the girl finally got the shoes off. Yet, the girl could think of nothing but the bewitching dancing shoes.

The old woman became ill. Unfortunately, this occurred at the same time a grand ball was in town. Instead of staying with the old woman, the girl decided to show off her shoes at the ball. But again, when she started to dance, the shoes wouldn't stop. At first she was enchanted by the dancing and loved being able to do so many steps. But hours went by and she began to tire. She wished she could stop. Her feet ached and she could hardly breathe. She saw the old soldier's face in the sky, mocking her with the refrain "Such beautiful dancing shoes."

The shoes took her by the church door, where she saw a stern angel with a sword. He cursed her, telling her she must dance until she was too tired to dance anymore, to show all the vain and proud children their folly. She danced and danced, at one point passing by the funeral of the kind old woman. When she couldn't dance anymore, she begged the angel to cut off her feet. He did so, and also taught her to be repentant.

The girl tried three times to go to church so that she could be forgiven. The first two times she had self-pity and revenge in her heart, and was turned back each time by visions of the red shoes. Finally, she returned home honestly repentant. She was taken in by the parson's wife, and became a good model for the other children. The angel appeared before her again and magically brought her to church, where she was forgiven. Her heart broke and her soul flew to heaven.

How to Tell This Story

This is primarily a religious tale; you can make it as religious or secular as you desire. Perhaps the red shoes were a new pair of Air Jordans that the girl decided to wear to a fancy family get-together. The spooky soldier, now maybe a creepy rich stranger, could have cursed the shoes by putting magic gold laces on them, which forced the child to slam-dunk all day. Then you can limit the gore by just cutting off the laces to save her. Be sure to make the old soldier character memorable, with certain details—maybe a curly red beard, a flashing gold tooth, or a shiny black car.

For almost all young children it's probably best to change the plot considerably so that the girl gets the shoes off by performing some deed of atonement and then comes home to be with the old woman.

Rip Van Winkle

Summary

In this Washington Irving story, Rip Van Winkle was a time traveler of sorts, but rather than make use of his knowledge, he preferred to continue as he always was. The story is simple. Rip Van Winkle, a kindly, lazy, henpecked man, set out for a remote part of the Catskill Mountains. He fell asleep and woke up twenty years later. Things were strange to him, and it took a while for him to realize what had happened. He had slept through the Revolution. Rip Van Winkle just continued being his old self, not worrying about politics or the world outside.

The Characters

Rip Van Winkle: Disdained work, but was willing to help a friend or neighbor anytime. Had his gun, his dog, and his way of doing things, and could be content fishing all day, even if he didn't catch anything. Had a pleasant disposition.

Dame Van Winkle: Ruler of the Van Winkle household, center of the town's gossip.

Young Rip Van Winkle: The bets were that he would be a duplicate of his father.

Other characters: When Rip awoke, he met a large number of people; their individual characters aren't crucial to the story.

The Plot

Before the Revolution, Rip Van Winkle lived in a small village of Dutch colonists at the foot of the Catskill Mountains.

Rip lived his life as he wanted—he hardly worked (he was a farmer), he fished a lot, and he was helpful to his friends. And he was an obedient husband. He loved playing with children, and they loved playing with him. Rip Van Winkle was a descendant of the Van Winkles from Peter Stuyvesant's time; those Van Winkles had fought bravely, but this Van Winkle wasn't interested in that at all. He hated work.

Two centuries ago, the Catskills were a beautiful place—and they still are. Gentle mountains, crisp streams, lush valleys—the Catskills were among the most beautiful places in the colonies.

Rip Van Winkle's farm stood in sharp contrast to the Catskills. It was unkempt and messy. But this was the way he liked it.

In the evenings there would be discussions at the home of Nicholas Vedder, a village leader and innkeeper. Dame Van Winkle thought these meetings contributed to Rip Van Winkle's slothfulness, because all he had to do was sit around, and she told Vedder so.

After some time, Rip Van Winkle could no longer stand the nagging. He went for a walk one afternoon with his dog, Wolf. He wandered a bit, and when it grew dark, he decided that it would be best to go home. As he descended, he heard someone shouting, "Rip Van Winkle! Rip Van Winkle!" But he saw no one.

Rip wandered down the hill. He saw an oddly dressed stranger, wearing old Dutch clothing. He helped the stranger carry a keg up the mountain. Rip couldn't figure out why this man would want to carry a keg up the mountain. When they got to the top, Rip found an amphitheater, in which the oddest-looking people were playing ninepins (bowling). These people were of all sizes; they all wore pants too big for them; they all had beards. The stranger poured the keg's contents into a flask, called a flagon.

Rip was offered a drink, which he enjoyed. He drank so much that he fell asleep. When he awoke, it was morning. He couldn't imagine that he had slept all night. "Now I'm in trouble," he thought. "What excuse shall I make to Dame Van Winkle?"

He found his gun, but it was rusted through. Rip suspected that those men had stolen his gun and replaced it with this rusty one. Wolf was gone, too. Rip went to look for the amphitheater, but it was gone. So he decided to head back to his village.

When he arrived at the village, there were only strangers. Clothing had changed fashion. He didn't recognize any of the children or any of the dogs, either. There were new houses, and his house was falling apart and empty.

On the main street he saw a sign: "The Union Hotel, Proprietor Jonathan Doolittle." But Nicholas Vedder owned the hotel! A picture of King George was still there, but it, too, was different. Underneath this picture was the name "General Washington."

Rip rubbed his chin, and noticed that he had a long, scraggly beard. Because of his odd appearance, people gathered around him. Somebody asked whether Rip was a "Federal or Democrat," and Rip replied, "I am a loyal subject of the king."

People shouted, "A Tory, a spy! Away with him!"

Somebody restored order. Rip assured the man that he meant no harm, but was just looking for his neighbors. The man asked, "Who are your neighbors?"

Rip said, "Nicholas Vedder."

The man replied that Vedder had died years ago.

Rip went through a whole list of names—all of them had completed their lives years ago.

Rip finally asked if anyone knew Rip Van Winkle, and somebody pointed to Rip's son and said, "Rip Van Winkle is over there." Rip saw a slothful, ragged-looking man, an image of himself as he had looked when he went up the mountain.

A woman, Judith Gardener, appeared and told the younger Rip, who was, like his father, a little agitated about this, to hush. Rip questioned her, and she said that her father was

Rip Van Winkle. "He left home twenty years ago—when I was a little girl—with his dog and was never seen again."

Rip finally realized what had happened. "I'm your father," he exclaimed.

Rip then told his story. Everyone agreed that the Catskills were indeed haunted by strange beings. It was rumored that Henry Hudson, the great explorer, and his crew played ninepins in the mountains every twenty years.

Rip resumed his old ways. He fished, helped friends with various tasks like cutting down cherry trees, hunted, and made friends. But he never did work for a living; that wasn't his way.

Whenever there's thunder in the Catskills, it may be Henry Hudson and his crew that you hear.

How to Tell This Story

"Rip Van Winkle" is a simple story but has many possible variations. Here are some:

Every time Rip fell asleep in the mountains he woke up twenty years later; a traveler through history. This would be an interesting way to teach your children some of the more important events in American history.

Who else was wandering the Catskill mountains? Perhaps some important figures from American history?

If you've been to the Catskills (and even if you haven't), the tale offers an excellent opportunity to describe wildlife and scenery.

Because this story spans the American Revolution, there's plenty of opportunity to talk about that key event.

Finally, children are going to be interested in the details—what Rip's dog was like, what Rip looked like, what the ninepin players were like, what the townspeople did. This story, though a fantasy, offers a chance to introduce your children to what American life was like in the 1700s.

The Robber Bridegroom

Summary

A miller's daughter was married against her will to a robber. The robber planned to take her to his evil band of murderers, kill her, and then eat her. The girl discovered the plot, then caused the robber and his band to be caught and executed for their crimes.

The Characters

The miller: A good man who, unfortunately, was not such a good judge of character.

The miller's daughter: A clever and beautiful girl; she resisted the marriage because she didn't trust the robber.

The robber bridegroom: Seemed to be rich and suitable, but was truly evil.

The old woman: A servant kept by the robber in his cellar. She was kind and helped the miller's daughter escape.

The robber's band: All equally evil, this disgusting bunch eat human flesh.

The Plot

The miller promised his daughter to the robber bridegroom, believing that the man was rich and upstanding. His daughter resisted the marriage, but had to go to meet her intended groom at his house. She did not trust him, so she scattered peas on the way to his house to mark her way back.

She reached the house, where a bird in a cage sang to her to turn back.

The bride could not find anyone home until she ventured into the cellar. There she found an old woman, who warned her that her bridegroom was really a murderous monster. This was a murderer's den, she told the girl, and if she remained she would be killed and eaten. The old woman helped the bride hide. That evening she saw the bridegroom and his murderous gang bring home a young girl, whom they killed with three glasses of poisonous wine. One of the robbers tried to steal a ring from the girl's finger but couldn't get it off, so he chopped off the finger. The finger flew through the air and landed in the bride's lap in her hiding place. The old woman stalled the robbers in their search for the ring and gave them wine with sleeping medicine. The woman then escaped with the bride. They found their way back by following the peas.

When the wedding day arrived, the guests and the robber gathered to tell stores. The miller's daughter told the story of her fearful trip to her evil groom's house. When she came to the part about the finger, she produced the real finger that had landed in her lap. The robber bridegroom tried to escape, but was caught. He and his murderous fellows were executed.

How to Tell This Story

This gruesome story could be changed to make it less gory and scary. The robber bridegroom could be a drug pusher instead of a homicidal cannibal, for instance. Maybe he was after the girl's jewelry. The ring could fly off with the finger intact. No matter how you tell it, the important message is that the miller should not have been fooled by the robber's riches—looks can be deceiving.

Robin Hood and the Merry Woman

Summary

There are many Robin Hood stories. In this one, Robin Hood was being chased by the bishop through the forest. He ran into an old woman's house. They changed clothes, so that the bishop captured the woman, and Robin Hood escaped. Later Robin Hood rejoined his men in the forest and they captured the bishop.

The Characters

Robin Hood: A scoundrel and a thief, but good-hearted. He stole from the rich to give to the poor. He was wanted by the king and the bishop, but loved by poor people.

The merry old woman: Looking for adventure; adventure found her. She liked to spin yarn, sing, and dance. She's only old chronologically.

The bishop: He wanted nothing more than to capture his nemesis, Robin Hood, and to present Robin Hood to the king for a reward.

Robin Hood's band: In this story, the particular personalities of the various characters in Robin Hood's band aren't important to know. They included Much, Little John, Friar Tuck, and Will Scarlet.

The Plot

Robin Hood took refuge in the house of a merry old woman, who, when she first saw him, thought that he was a robber. When she recognized him she was thrilled and invited Robin Hood in. Robin Hood told the merry woman that the bishop was after him. Robin Hood wanted to hide in a hidden room or metal chest or featherbed, but the old woman had no such thing.

She remembered last winter when Robin Hood and his gang had brought her firewood to keep her warm—he had saved her from the bitter cold.

She suggested to Robin Hood that they switch clothing and that Robin Hood work at the spinning wheel. She showed Robin Hood what to do. (He was a thief, not a clothmaker.)

Soon after, the bishop burst into her house looking for Robin Hood. When the bishop asked the woman at the spinning wheel (who was really Robin Hood) if she had seen Robin Hood, the woman remained silent (talking would reveal her identity). The bishop took the woman, disguised as Robin Hood, into his coach.

The merry old woman had a hard time not laughing as they carried her into the coach.

When the bishop was gone, Robin Hood dashed out of the house to rejoin his men. As Robin Hood was looking for his men, they saw what they thought was a witch walking through the woods. (Robin Hood didn't really look much like a woman, even an old one.) Much, Little John, Friar Tuck, and Will Scarlet talked about how important it was to kill a witch, not just wound her with an arrow, lest the shooter be cursed. Just as Much was about to shoot Robin Hood, Friar Tuck shouted, "Wait, it's Master Robin."

Meanwhile, the bishop was boasting about capturing Robin Hood. Suddenly, he saw men on horses approaching. "Who's that?" he asked. The woman replied, "I think it's Robin Hood and his men."

"Who are you?" the bishop asked the woman with surprise in his voice.

Robin Hood captured the bishop. The merry old woman stayed with Robin Hood's men for a while and had a wonderful time singing and dancing. The next day, Robin Hood put the woman on his best horse and led her home. When she arrived home, the merry old woman laughed at what Robin Hood had spun—a single, long thread.

How to Tell This Story

Details—add details. Describe the merry old woman's house. Talk about the clothes that Robin Hood put on. Describe a spinning wheel—you can bet that most children have never seen one.

There's plenty of dialogue you can incorporate into this story, as well. Conversations between the woman and Robin Hood, between the woman and the bishop, and among Robin Hood's men, for example.

Robin Hood's role in society is the foundation of the Robin Hood stories. Why did he steal from the rich to give to the poor? Was this good?

Despite the drama—the bishop was intent on capturing Robin Hood—the story has humor. For children, the idea of men dressing up as women and vice versa is very funny.

Sirens

Summary

This is an elegant, urban story, designed simply to calm nighttime fears that your child may have from hearing sirens. Police cars, ambulances, fire engines—all can send a cold chill down a small child's spine. There are no people or animals in this story. All "Sirens" does is explain what those noises are and offer reassurance. To an eighteen-month-old to three-year-old, "Sirens" can turn scary sounds into comforting characters.

The Characters

A fire engine, an ambulance, and a police car.

The Plot

There is not really a plot. You say: We like to hear sirens because that means someone's getting help. When you hear a siren, that means a police car, a fire engine, or an ambulance is going somewhere.

The police car comes to help you when you're lost and need a ride home. And it makes a siren noise when it comes: "Whoo, whoo, whoo."

The ambulance takes people to the hospital when they're sick. The hospital makes people feel all better. When the ambulance comes, it makes a siren noise: "Whoo, whoo, whoo."

The fire engine comes to put out fires and save lives. The fire engine also rescues cats that get stuck in trees. When the fire engine comes, it makes a siren noise: "Whoo, whoo, whoo."

How to Tell This Story

Tell "Sirens" when your child is frightened by sirens. But tell it also when there are no sirens around, so your child gets used to the story, and used to sirens. Adding this story to your repertoire will help immunize your child to the noisy, often frightening sound that police cars, ambulances, and fire engines make. If you get your child to make a "whoo, whoo, whoo" sound, you've come a long way toward eliminating a great fear.

Sleeping Beauty

Summary

This is a story of a kingdom that fell under a sleeping spell for one hundred years until a prince kissed Sleeping Beauty (the princess) and woke everybody up.

The king and queen had a party for the birth of their daughter; they invited all the fairies in the kingdom except one, whom they forgot. Each fairy gave the princess a gift. The forgotten fairy put a terrible spell on the princess. One fairy had not yet bestowed her gift, and although she could not undue the mean fairy's curse, she could change it, so that the princess would sleep for only one hundred years until a handsome prince kissed her.

The Characters

The king and queen: Both desperately wanted a child.

Sleeping Beauty: A nice girl; happy, too. She got her name, Sleeping Beauty, from all the people who told the story to ambitious princes who then tried to get into the castle to see the famed princess.

The fairies: The king invited twelve, but there were really thirteen. The fairies were all magical, mystical beings. The thirteenth fairy was rather frightening-looking, with a hooked nose and dark clothes.

The kingdom: This is an important entity. It was a city inside a castle, and when the princess pricked her finger up in the highest tower, all the people and creatures in the kingdom fell asleep no matter what they were doing.

The prince: Handsome; rides a horse.

The frog: A fortune-telling amphibian.

The Plot

A king and queen longed for a child. One day while the queen was bathing, a frog hopped out of her bath and told the queen that she would have a baby girl before the year's end. As predicted, the queen gave birth to a daughter, and the overjoyed parents decided to throw a feast in celebration, inviting all the nobles and the fairies in the land. Unfortunately, the king only knew about twelve fairies, although there were thirteen.

Everyone attended the feast, and the fairies presented the child with magical promises like "beauty," "goodness," "riches," "charm," and so on. Just after the eleventh fairy gave her gift, the thirteenth fairy appeared, furious that she was not invited.

The thirteenth fairy screamed in a frightening voice, "When the princess is fifteen, she will prick her finger on a spindle and die!" Everyone was horrified. Fortunately, the twelfth fairy had not yet presented her gift. She said, "I cannot remove the curse, but I can weaken it. The princess will not die; instead she will fall into a deep sleep that will last for one hundred years."

The king ordered all the spindles in the kingdom destroyed. On her fifteenth birthday, the parents went out (to a movie or flogging or something) and left the princess alone to explore the castle. She found a room off a hidden corridor.

Inside the room was an old woman with a spindle (who looked a lot like the thirteenth fairy, by the way). The princess had never seen a spindle and asked the woman what she was doing. The woman said, "I am spinning, my dear." The princess tried the spindle, but pricked her finger. Instantly, she fell on the bed in the room and went into a deep sleep.

The king and queen, who were just returning, fell asleep in the doorway, and all the members of the kingdom fell asleep in the middle of whatever they were doing. All the animals fell asleep too.

Over the years, a prickly briar hedge grew up along the

castle, which no one could penetrate. Hearing of the legend, many princes from other lands tried to pass through, but were killed by the thorns.

One hundred years later, a handsome and brave prince rode to the castle. The prince wasn't deterred when he heard of the many who had died trying to see Sleeping Beauty. When he approached the briar hedge, it melted away and became a flowering path. The prince walked past all the sleeping nobility and climbed the staircase to the room where Sleeping Beauty slept. He was nervous, but she was so beautiful he decided to kiss her. The princess, then the rest of the kingdom, woke up. The two lived happily ever after.

How to Tell This Story

You can shorten the story by summarizing the background— just say that the princess had had a curse put upon her by a mean fairy—and begin at the princess's fifteenth birthday. You could spend some time describing all the creatures who were stopped in their path by the spell. For example, describe the cook falling asleep by the stove and the fire burning out. Tell how the pigeons put their heads under their wings and the children stopped running through the castle. Then let them wake up and go back into action.

You might want to describe the kinds of flowers that began blooming on the path, or describe each of the fairies' costumes. In the original story, all were female, but you can mix it up. You can also describe the castle while the princess explored it.

Modernize this story by making Sleeping Beauty the daughter of a wealthy family who invited all the local merchants in to see the baby except the CEO of a pharmaceutical company. He could put a curse on her, and she could take an unidentified pill from the medicine chest and thus put the house and servants to sleep for years. Then a brilliant doctor visited after one hundred years (it took that long to get an appointment) and saved her with an operation.

Give Sleeping Beauty and the prince names. (Di and Charles are one possibility.)

Small Star and the Mud Pony

Summary

In this Native American story, Small Star desperately wanted a pony, but his family was poor. He built a corral in a hollow across the river and made two small ponies from mud. He cared for them daily. One of the ponies became real, and Small Star took the best care of him, and always covered him with a buffalo hide each night. The mud pony helped him become a skilled warrior with many horses. One day a new colt, the image of his mud pony, appeared among his herd, and in a dream his mud pony appeared to him and told him to care for the colt as if it were the mud pony. Then the mud pony returned to Mother Earth. The brave became a great chief, and he always took special care of his colt, which became a great horse.

The Characters

Small Star: His family was poor but loving. They had enough to eat, but no horses. Each day, Small Star watched with envy when the other boys in the Fish Hawk village rode and played with their horses.

Small Star's parents: They couldn't give their son what he wanted most.

The mud pony: A supernatural horse given life by the god Tirawa. The mud pony was the original talking horse, and this pony gave good advice.

The Plot

Small Star and his parents were quite poor, although their village was a comfortable one. All the other boys had ponies, and Small Star wanted one too, badly enough to build a corral in a hidden hollow near the river and to make two mud ponies there. One was dun-colored, like the mud, but he mixed red clay into the mud to make the other, and it was a sorrel. He put a white blaze across the sorrel's face with white clay. Every day he went to his mud ponies to take care of them; he patted them, gave them grass and cottonwood shoots, and talked to them all day long. At night he carefully closed the corral and went home. He didn't tell anyone about his mud ponies. One morning when Small Star went to water his ponies, the dun-colored pony had dried up and crumbled to dust. He took special care of the remaining one, and often slept with it in the corral.

One day while Small Star was tending his mud pony, a runner came into the village and announced that the buffalo were running, so it was time for the village to pick up and follow them for the summer hunt. The people packed up their tepees, food, and equipment in great excitement. Small Star's parents looked for him, and not finding him, assumed he was with the other children and set out on their way.

That night, Small Star returned to Fish Hawk village and found it empty. The earth lodges were stripped bare, the people and animals were gone, and he knew they had traveled fast and far on the summer buffalo hunt. He didn't know how he would find his family and friends again, and he was frightened. He searched and found some parched corn and jerky that the people had forgotten, and he ate it. Then he lay down in his family's old lodge and tried to sleep. HIs sleep was disturbed by dreams in which he was chasing his mud pony. In his dream, the voice of the Great Tirawa spoke to him and said he had noticed how Small Star loved and cared for the mud pony. Then Tirawa promised to help Small Star and told him to continue caring for the mud pony.

Small Star slept fitfully the rest of the night, and in the morning took water and grass to the mud pony first thing. That night he slept in the corral beside the horse. The mud pony spoke to Small Star in his dreams and told him Mother Earth had taken pity on him, and if Small Star did as the pony told him, all would be well. Then the pony told him he would one day be chief.

In the morning the mud pony was gone. But outside the corral stood a fine sorrel with a white blaze across his face. Small Star couldn't believe his good luck and ran to the horse. As he stood beside the horse, he promised the Great Tirawa he would remember his words and do as he wished. When he led the pony to the river to drink, the pony told him he would take him to his people, and so Small Star didn't need to direct him as he rode.

They traveled through the day and reached the first campsite of the people of Fish Hawk village. The horse foraged while Small Star searched the campsite for forgotten food. He slept next to his pony. And so they continued for three more days. At sunset on the third day, they reached the fourth campsite, and the coals were still warm, so Small Star knew they were close. The pony told him to leave him and go to his family, but to return to him the next morning. His parents rejoiced when they saw him, and in the morning, other villagers came to join in the rejoicing. As soon as he could, Small Star returned to the sorrel, and they followed the traveling villagers at a distance. They continued like this for several days until one day the pony told Small Star it was time for the villagers to know he had a horse, so Small Star should take him into the camp that night. He also said the chief would offer Small Star four horses for him, and that Small Star should accept the offer.

Sure enough, the village chief wanted to trade for the sorrel and was quite pleased with his trade. The mud pony appeared to Small Star in a dream and told him to tan a buffalo hide and use it to cover him each night. Small Star tanned a hide and carefully covered the pony each night. On the day of the buffalo hunt, the mud pony performed marvelously. The chief was pleased with his response and speed, but then the pony came up lame when he stumbled.

The ungrateful chief demanded his four horses back and returned the injured pony to Small Star. Then the chief insulted him and the pony, saying the animal looked just like a mud pony. From then on, Small Star was known as Mud-Pony-Boy. Mud-Pony-Boy healed the horse with loving care and herbal compresses for the injured foot. Of course, then the chief wanted the pony back, but Mud-Pony-Boy would not agree.

One day an enemy tribe attacked the village. The pony told Mud-Pony-Boy to cover himself with mud the same color as the pony's sorrel coat and to go into battle that way. The mud would protect him from warrior arrows. Mud-Pony-Boy triumphed in battle, and the villagers recognized him as a brave, not a boy, after that day.

Soon after the battle, the villagers returned to their permanent earth-lodge village. It was the fall, and corn-harvesting time, but an enemy tribe attacked them before they could get ready for the coming winter. One of the enemy warriors was protected by the spirit of the Turtle, and no one could hurt him. Mud-Pony-Boy observed him in battle and saw he could be wounded under his arm, so he waited until the enemy warrior raised his arm to shoot an arrow. Then he thrust his lance into the vulnerable spot and killed the warrior.

Through the years, Mud-Pony-Boy continued to distinguish himself in battle, and he took many horses and did many brave things. He became recognized as the successor to the chief. But no matter how good things were for him, Mud-Pony-Boy never forgot to cover his pony with the buffalo hide.

One day a sorrel colt with a star blaze on his head appeared in Mud-Pony-Boy's corral, and that night, after years of silence, the mud pony spoke to him in a dream. The sorrel told Mud-Pony-Boy it was time for him to go, but he was leaving the colt to take his place. He should love the colt as he loved the mud pony.

A storm arose that night, and Mud-Pony-Boy couldn't find his mud pony when he went to cover him with the buffalo hide.

The next morning, he returned to the old corral of his child-hood and found a mound of mud with a blaze of white. The voice of the pony came to him and told him not to be sad be-cause they had enjoyed their time together. The mud pony had returned to Mother Earth and was content. He predicted Mud-Pony-Boy would be chief and the colt would grow into a great horse. And he was right.

How to Tell This Story

This tale gives you a good chance to introduce traditional Native American culture to your child. Spend some time estab-lishing a lifestyle for Small Star. His family was poor, probably because his father was ill and couldn't hunt. They didn't have much to eat, but they loved each other. Others in the village were kind to them, but they weren't rich enough to be generous and share. In the winter, the villagers stayed in permanent earth lodges in Fish Hawk village, and in the summer, they fol-lowed the herds of buffalo and hunted to provision themselves for the winter. Before they left on the hunt, the women planted crops that would be ready for harvest when they returned from the hunt. In the fall, the women also had to dry meat to eat dur-ing the winter. The villagers often had ceremonies to honor the Great Tirawa, and they danced and feasted long into the night. Small Star had a wonderful life and would have been perfectly content if he only had had a pony like other boys in the village. They took their ponies out riding during the day, but not all of them were kind to their animals. Small Star knew he would treat a pony better than any of the boys did.

During the long winters, the people gathered around fires in the lodges and told stories. The women sewed moccasins and shirts and decorated clothes with fringe and quillwork. The people played games to pass the time during the winter too. In conjunction with this story, you might try some activi-ties to teach your child more about traditional Native Ameri-can lifestyles. Play some Native American games, make a tepee in the backyard, or eat some foods Small Star enjoyed—beef jerky would be a close approximation.

The Snow Queen

Summary

This is the story of a little girl, Gerda, and her quest to find and bring home her lost and bewitched playmate, Kay (pronounced to rhyme with "eye"—Kay is a boy). Kay was hurt by two pieces of glass from a demon's mirror—one in his eye that caused him to see the worst in everything, and one in his heart that caused his heart to turn to ice. He left his village with the icy Snow Queen, whom he cannot recognize because of his condition. Gerda had many adventures searching for Kay, finally rescuing him and returning home with him.

The Characters

Gerda: The star of the story, Gerda was successful in her quest to find Kay because of her honesty and her innocence. She was aided by people, animals, and plants, who were all charmed by her devotion to Kay.

Kay: Gerda's next-door playmate, a boy, poisoned by glass from the demon's mirror. He went with the Snow Queen under this spell, but did not realize his peril because he was enchanted by the icy Snow Queen. Kay is good and kind at heart, but acts mean-spirited because of the spell.

The old grandmother: A minor character, the old grandmother told Gerda and Kay stories when they were playmates, and shares the morale of the story.

The Snow Queen: While the Snow Queen was the villain of the story because she lured Kay away, she was not so much evil as lonely and manipulative. Her icy, delicate beauty entranced Kay. She resided in a castle made of ice and snow, and her legions were huge snowflakes come to life.

The magical flower woman: One of the people Gerda met on her journey, the old magical woman enchanted Gerda and caused her to forget Kay and her mission. The benign old woman wore a big flowered garden hat and tended a magical flower garden.

The crow: The talking crow sent Gerda to the prince and princess.

The prince and princess: The prince was mistaken for Kay. The kind, generous pair were moved by Gerda's story.

The little robber girl: A feisty and spoiled robber girl, she kept many animal pets but mistreated them.

The Lapp woman and the Finn woman: These kind old women directed Gerda to the palace of the Snow Queen.

The Plot

The tale of the Snow Queen opens with the breaking of the demon mirror. A demon created a mirror that distorted all reflections so that everything bad or strange stood out and everything good or innocent couldn't be seen. His servant demons intended to fly to heaven to mock the angels with their mirror, but they dropped the mirror, which fell to earth and broke into millions of pieces. Pieces from the mirror occasionally got into people's eyes, distorting their perception, or into their hearts, turning their hearts to ice.

Enter Kay and Gerda. The two playmates lived next door to each other in a small village, and spent their time with each other or with the old grandmother listening to stories under their joining rose trees. One day while they were sharing stories, Kay got a shard of the demon mirror in one eye and another in his heart. Despite her efforts, Gerda could not help Kay, and he began to treat her badly. Later that winter, as Kay was sledding in the big square, he attached his sled to a bigger white sled, which drove him away. It was the Snow Queen's sled—and Kay disappeared.

After much searching, the village people gave Kay up for dead. Gerda was informed by the sunshine and the swallows that Kay was still alive. So she left in search of him, taking her favorite red shoes. She threw her shoes into the river as an offering for Kay's return, but they floated back to her, signaling that the river could not help her. Gerda floated down the river in a boat that happened by, and was brought back to shore by the magical flower woman.

The magical flower woman wanted to keep little Gerda with her, so she entranced Gerda by combing Gerda's hair with a magic comb, causing Gerda to forget Kay and her search. Then the woman cleared out all the roses from her garden so that Gerda would not remember her home. But the magical flower woman forgot to remove the painted roses from her garden hat. When Gerda noticed these, she became homesick and nearly abandoned her mission. As she cried, the garden roses sprang out of the ground from beneath her tears. She then asked each of several types of flowers in turn if they knew where Kay was, but they only answered with stories of things that they themselves had witnessed. Gerda finally ran away in desperation.

A crow found Gerda alone, and after hearing of her search for Kay, offered to help. The crow told Gerda of the princess who would only marry a man who could speak well. In the crow's story, a simple boy met the challenge because of his lack of pomp and his courage, and married the princess. Since the crow believed that this was Kay, the crow and Gerda traveled to the castle. Gerda found that it was not Kay, but the prince and princess were so taken with her story that they gave Gerda fine clothes and a carriage to help her in her search.

The carriage was later attacked by a band of robbers, who killed everyone in it except little Gerda, who was saved by a little robber girl because she wanted a playmate. The robber girl took Gerda's nice clothes and kept her captive.

She showed Gerda her collection of captured pets, including two wood pigeons and a reindeer. The pigeons informed Gerda that the Snow Queen had Kay in her palace in Lapland, where the reindeer was from. When Gerda told this to the robber girl, the girl felt sorry for Gerda and helped her escape. The robber girl gave Gerda the reindeer, and off they went to Lapland.

Gerda and the reindeer encountered a Lapp woman, who gave them food and directions to the Finn woman—the Finn woman lived close to the Snow Queen. She directed them to the Snow Queen's palace. Outside the palace, Gerda was attacked by huge snowflakes, but they were repelled by angels that materialized from Gerda's cold breath.

Once inside the Snow Queen's freezing palace, Gerda found Kay drawing nonsense patterns with ice on the floor. The Snow Queen was away. Gerda approached Kay, who was blue with cold but oblivious to his predicament because of the ice in his heart. Gerda hugged him and cried hot tears, which melted the piece of mirror that had turned Kay's heart to ice. Then Kay, recognizing Gerda, cried as well, washing out the mirror shard in his eye. Gerda kissed Kay, giving him back his strength.

On their way back, they ran into the robber girl on the way, who gave them news of the crow and the prince and princess. They finally reached home, and upon entering their grandmother's room, discovered that they were years older, but still children at heart.

How to Tell This Story

This long story can be shortened by eliminating some of the steps in Gerda's journey and just keeping in the necessary ingredients—such as the reindeer and the pigeons.

On the other hand, since each step in Gerda's journey makes a good story in itself, it can be equally effective to serialize this particular fairy tale. Will your child enjoy a story told over several days? There's only one way to find out. If you serialize, then add plenty of details. For instance, the section where Gerda was entranced by the magical flower woman can be stretched out to include lengthy descriptions of her cottage, her garden, or her person. You can stretch the stories told by each of the types of flowers, using exotic, made-up details of their places of origin or of things the flowers witnessed before. Perhaps the flower ancestors of the tiger lily were once flowers in the Taj Mahal, in a room with orange silk pillows and shiny mosaic floors. Each section of this story can be lengthened out this way, and you can end by cutting back briefly to Kay's doings in the Snow Queen's palace to keep up their interest in the overall story.

This tale can be brought up to date by making Kay a hotshot snowboarder and putting the Snow Queen in a superpowered snowmobile. The evil mirror can be changed to an evil spy satellite that broke up in the atmosphere, spreading radioactive infective particles on the village. Gerda could be searching for Kay to give him the therapy injection that will save him from the mutation disease.

Snow White and the Seven Dwarfs

Summary

This tale is about a jealous stepmother who plotted to kill Snow White, a gorgeous young girl. It is also about the seven dwarfs who loved, protected, and cared for the girl. The evil queen vainly tried to be the prettiest ("fairest") in the land. To determine the reigning beauty, she consulted her omniscient talking mirror. She tried many different ways to kill Snow White, but was unsuccessful. A prince from a neighboring kingdom saved Snow White and married her.

The Characters

Snow White: The king and first queen's very attractive daughter. She had shiny black hair, skin as white as snow, and cheeks as red as the setting sun. She was beautiful and sweet but very naive.

The queen: Birth mother of Snow White, she wished for this beautiful child but soon died.

The king: A no-show in this story—doesn't have a line and doesn't protect his daughter from his nasty new wife.

The evil queen: Snow White's stepmother was jealous, vain, and cruel.

The seven dwarfs: Very kind, intelligent, industrious, clean creatures who loved Snow White.

The huntsman: A hunter with a big heart.

The prince: Quintessential prince who always got what he wanted.

The servant: Clumsy, but he saved the day.

The Plot

The story opens with a queen sitting by her open bedroom window sewing a tapestry (embroidered picture made into a wall hanging) on a frame of black ebony. There was snow falling outside. The queen pricked her finger and thought that the red drops of blood looked so beautiful against the snowflakes that she would like a child with the same coloring: skin as white as snow, rosy red cheeks, and hair as black as ebony. Of course, her wish came true, and she named her child Snow White.

Sadly, the queen died one year later. The king waited a year before he married a beautiful, proud woman. The new queen could not bear anyone to be as beautiful as she and regularly checked with her magic talking mirror, asking,

> "*Mirror, mirror on the wall,*
> *Who is the fairest one of all?*"

The mirror always answered,

"My fair queen, you are the fairest of them all."

One day, when Snow White was older, the mirror informed the queen:

"Queen, you are so fair, 'tis true,
  But Snow White is a hundred times fairer than you."

This upset the queen, and she decided to have Snow White killed. She called her huntsman in and ordered him to take Snow White into the forest, kill her, and bring back her heart. The huntsman did take Snow White into the forest, but when she cried, he couldn't kill her. The huntsman killed a wild boar and cut out its heart. When the queen saw the heart she cooked it and rejoiced, believing that the girl was dead.

Snow White came upon a small cottage in the mountains. Everything in the cottage was unusually small and clean. She saw seven place settings and seven beds with white sheets. She took a sip of wine from every cup and a bite of bread from every plate, so she didn't take everything from any one setting. She fell asleep on one of the beds.

Later, the owners returned: seven dwarfs who worked in the mountains digging for diamonds. In unison they exclaimed, "What a beautiful girl." When Snow White woke up the next day, she told them her story.

The dwarfs said she could stay in exchange for housework. The dwarfs warned Snow White that her stepmother would soon find out she was alive, so she must never to let anyone in the cottage while they were gone.

The queen hadn't checked her mirror since she cooked the heart. One day, she did ask and was told:

"Queen, you are still fair, 'tis true,
  But in the cottage where the seven dwarfs stay,
  Snow White is a hundred times fairer than you!"

The queen was livid. She schemed to kill the child herself.

The queen disguised herself as a peddler and traveled through the mountains to the cottage. She knocked on the door while Snow White was alone. The peddler in disguise showed Snow White her beautiful, colorful laces. Snow White was enchanted and welcomed in the disguised queen. The queen tied Snow White so tightly with the laces that she fainted.

When the dwarfs returned, they untied the laces so she was able to breathe again. Again, they admonished her not to let anyone in. They said the peddler was her wicked stepmother.

Back at the palace, the queen asked the mirror the usual question. The mirror again told her Snow White was "a thousand times fairer than you," which outraged the queen. She plotted a new method to kill Snow White: with a poisoned comb. The queen traveled back to the cottage again in a disguise, but this time, Snow White told her to go away. The "peddler" showed her the comb and told Snow White that she, the peddler, would place it properly in her hair. Snow White let her, then collapsed.

Again the dwarfs resuscitated Snow White. Again the queen's mirror informed her that Snow White was still fairer. This time, the queen prepared a breathtaking poison apple. One side of the apple was white and had no poison. The rosy side had the poison. Anyone who saw this apple would crave a bite.

The queen showed up at the cottage again dressed as an old farm woman, and Snow White told her that she was not interested in buying any apples. The queen said she would give her one, and would prove it was not poison by eating half of it. Snow White watched the "old farm woman" eat half and thought the apple was safe. She bit into the bad side and died. The queen laughed, saying, "Now even seven dwarfs can't save you!" Later at the palace, the mirror confirmed that there was no one fairer than the queen.

The dwarfs were devastated, because they could not figure out how to save Snow White this time. She looked very beautiful still, so they decided to bury her in a glass coffin and place it in the mountains, where one dwarf would always stand guard. They engraved her name in gold and wrote on the plaque that she was the daughter of a king. For many years she lay in the coffin, but strangely remained as lovely as if she were still alive.

One day a prince passed by the cottage and glanced up the hill. He saw the coffin and was enraptured. The prince asked the dwarfs if he could have the coffin, saying he would pay anything for it. The dwarfs declined, saying no gold or silver would let them part with it. The prince said, "Then give her to me as a present, because I cannot live without looking on her. I promise to love and cherish her as the person dearest in the world to me." The dwarfs agreed.

The prince kissed Snow White—and she woke up. Snow White asked where she was, and the prince replied with joy that she was safe with him. He told her what had happened and asked her to marry him. Snow White said yes.

(In another version of the story, one of the prince's servants tripped, and the coffin broke open on the ground. The piece of apple in Snow White's mouth was jarred loose, and she woke up.)

The wedding feast was announced throughout the land, and the wicked stepmother planned to attend, not knowing that it would be Snow White's wedding. The wicked queen wore her finest clothes of gold and silver. Her mirror, ever truthful, told her that "the young princess is a hundred times fairer than you." The queen was afraid to attend the wedding after hearing that, but curiosity got the better of her. When she saw that the new bride was Snow White, her evil heart swelled with passion and burst.

With no one left to sabotage them, Snow White and the prince lived happily ever after.

How to Tell This Story

Most children will learn and enjoy the mirror's answers. You may want to embellish the walk through the woods and the dwarfs' house, and even name the dwarfs. This story emphasizes how important it is to be wary of strangers.

One concern I have with many of these stories is that they portray stepparents as evil, plotting and jealous of their stepchildren. Perhaps you could change the relationship of this evil character from stepmother to a distant relative or a queen of no relation.

Snow White is a classic tale, one that conjures up wonderful images of mythical creatures. There's no need to update this story, because everyone from the adorable and bright little dwarfs to the noble huntsman is pure fantasy. Be sure to wrap your storytelling in magic and mystery.

If you do want to modernize it, however, have Snow White put the prince through some kind of test before she agrees to marry him.

The Straw Ox

Summary

The wife of a poor farmer told her husband to make her a straw ox, covered with tar. The husband was dubious, but went ahead anyway. On subsequent days, a bear, a wolf, a fox, and a rabbit tried to eat the straw ox, but became stuck to the ox. They were captured by the farmer, and in return for freedom they fetch the farmer and his wife valuable things—honey, sheep, hens and geese, and carrots and cauliflower.

The Characters

The farmer: Poor, hardworking, and compassionate, but not very imaginative.

The wife of the farmer: Poor, hardworking, and a little more imaginative than her husband.

The bear, the wolf, and the fox: Dumb animals, but not entirely stupid. While they fell for a trick, they were cunning enough to avoid being killed.

The Plot

A poor farmer and his wife lived in Russia. One day the wife told her husband to make an ox out of straw, cover it with tar, and put it in the field. She did not tell her husband why.

The next day a bear appeared and demanded to know what the ox was. The ox replied, "I am an ox made of straw and covered with tar." The bear didn't believe the ox and took a bite, but found himself stuck to the ox. The bear dragged the ox away for a bit; when the wife looked in the field she thought the ox had wandered away.

Then she saw the bear stuck to the sticky ox. She yelled for her husband to kill the bear; instead he threw the bear into the cellar.

The next day the same thing happened to a wolf. Then the following morning a fox was tricked by the ox; then a rabbit.

The day after all these animals were trapped in the cellar, the bear saw the farmer sharpening his knife. "Why?" the bear asked.

"To skin you and make bearskin jackets for me and my wife," the farmer replied.

"If you let me go," the bear said, "I'll bring you lots of honey." And so the farmer let him go.

The wolf then wanted to know why the farmer was sharpening his knife. "To skin you and make warm winter caps," the farmer replied. The wolf offered to get the farmer a herd of sheep if he let him go.

Then the fox wanted to know why the farmer was sharpening his knife. "To make a collar with your fur," the farmer replied. The fox offered to bring the farmer hens and geese.

Finally, the rabbit wanted to know about his fate. "To make mittens," the farmer replied. "How about some carrots and cauliflower for letting me go?" the rabbit suggested.

So all the animals went their way. A few nights later, the husband and his wife were awakened by scratching on the door. The animals had kept their promise and brought the farmer and his wife plenty of animals and food.

Eventually the straw-stuffed ox was weathered into small pieces.

How to Tell This Story

How many animals can you think of? That's how long "The Straw Ox" can get. It's fun to let your child think of animals, too.

There's a certain amount of suspense in this tale. Does the farmer kill the animals? Do the animals keep their promise? These are questions that you know the answers to, but your audience doesn't. And they are answers that require some explanation. So feel free to fill your children with lessons and morals from this story.

The Straw, the Coal, and the Bean

Summary

A straw, a coal, and a bean escaped the fire and set off for a foreign country. The straw and coal met a bad end in a running stream, and the bean, amused by their demise, laughed until it split its sides. A compassionate tailor sewed the bean's halves together again, and to this day, beans have a black seam.

The Characters

A straw: Long and thin.
A coal: Red-hot.
A bean: Uncooked.
A tailor: Quick with needle and thread.

The Plot

A poor village woman wanted to cook a dish of beans, so she built a fire with a handful of straw. A single bean, a straw, and a coal escaped. They agreed they were quite lucky to escape the fire and set off for a foreign country.

Soon they came to a stream with no bridge, and so the straw agreed to serve as a bridge for its two comrades. The coal went first, and as it was still quite hot, it burned through the straw in midstream, and they both fell into the water.

The bean found the sight amusing and laughed until its sides split, and it would have died, too, but a kindhearted tailor soon came along and sewed the two halves together with black thread. And that's why the bean has a black seam today.

How to Tell This Story

Stories explaining the appearance of everyday objects and animals are common to most storytelling traditions, and this is just one example. Tell this little story one day when you're serving beans, and they'll be more interesting. Make up your own stories about household objects.

Sweetheart Roland

Summary

A girl escaped with her sweetheart, Roland, from her foster mother, an evil witch who wanted to kill her. Her sweetheart then left her to go and prepare for the wedding, but he met another woman and forgot his first love. Later, the girl went to sing at Roland's wedding to his new love. Roland heard her voice again, remembered all that had happened, and fell for his first love. They then got married.

The Characters

The witch: A truly evil woman, she kept magic boots and a magic wand.

The evil daughter: Like her mother, truly evil, but also ugly.

April: The good foster daughter. Beautiful, and true to her sweetheart Roland.

Roland: Not especially noteworthy, but notably forgetful when it came to his first love.

The shepherd: Befriended April, when she was forgotten by Roland.

The Plot

A long time ago, a witch had an evil and ugly daughter and a good and beautiful foster daughter. The ugly evil daughter was jealous of her foster sister, and she and her witch mother schemed to murder the good child, April. The witch instructed the evil daughter to lie in her bed close to the wall, for the witch planned to chop off April's head with an ax while they slept in the same bed. April overheard the pair's plan, though, and changed places with her evil foster sister in the

the night. The witch thus ended up killing her favorite, the evil daughter.

April fled in the night to her sweetheart, Roland, begging him to help her escape the now enraged witch. He instructed her to steal the witch's magic wand to aid them in their escape. So April stole the wand, and also dropped three droplets of her sister's blood around the house. When the witch then came looking for her favorite daughter the next morning, the droplets of blood answered her, first on the stairs, then in the kitchen, and finally in the bedroom, where the witch found her favorite daughter dead by her own hand.

The witch was able to see her foster daughter and Roland fleeing because of her magic powers. So she slipped on her magic boots and took after them. But with the magic wand, the foster daughter turned Roland into a lake and herself into a duck in it, so that the witch was unable to reach them.

The next day, the witch approached the pair again, so Roland, who had magic powers, turned April into a rose in a briar patch and himself into a fiddler. Roland fiddled away on his magic fiddle, forcing the witch to dance. The witch danced away, unable to stop and unable to pluck the rose, until she died. Roland then removed the spell from himself and the good foster daughter. Roland then left to arrange their marriage, and April changed herself into a common red stone to avoid detection.

Unfortunately for April, when Roland went home he met another woman who made him forget his true love, so he did not return to fetch her. The despondent April changed herself into a flower, hoping that someone would step on her and put her out of her misery. A shepherd came by then, and was so enamored of the flower that he took it home and put it away safely in a chest.

The shepherd noticed that his house would magically tidy itself up before he awoke each morning. He consulted a wise woman, and she instructed him to throw a white cloth over whatever he saw moving in the morning in order to break the spell. The shepherd followed her instructions and discovered April, changed back from a flower. She confessed to cleaning his house, and also told her own sad tale. The shepherd wished to marry her, but she refused, wishing to remain faithful to her sweetheart, Roland.

Later, when the time for Roland's wedding had arrived, April was summoned with the rest of the maidens in the land to the wedding feast to sing for the pair. She tried to get out of it, but only succeeded in making herself the last to sing. When she finally sang to them, Roland remembered her and his love for her. He cried out that April was his true love, and they married there and then.

How to Tell This Story

This story is very adaptable in both length and content. If you wish to shorten it, you can simply leave out the last part and add another trial for the witch. The good foster daughter could use the wand to change Roland into an enormous tree and herself into a bird, thwarting the witch. You can add as many episodes like this as you like. For the shorter version, April and Roland could marry after the demise of the witch.

If you want to go with the longer version, you may want to elaborate more on why Roland so easily forgets about his true love. Maybe the ghost of the evil daughter bewitched him, or maybe the witch's wand erased his memory. Such a change might make Roland's forgetfulness more acceptable.

If you want to eliminate violence in the story, omit the switch with the evil daughter. The girl could simply escape without anyone else dying in her place.

The Tempest

Summary

Prospero, a duke deposed by his brother Antonio and the King of Naples, was left to die in a small boat with his daughter, Miranda. A lord of the court provisioned the boat, and so they survived until they landed on a deserted island. There Prospero learned magic, becoming an accomplished sorcerer. After twelve years, a ship passed the island, and the passengers included Antonio, the King of Naples, and his son, the crown prince, Ferdinand. Prospero used his powers to cause the passengers to be shipwrecked, and secured the ship safely in the harbor.

Miranda, who was by now quite grown up, fell in love with Ferdinand, and he asked her to marry him. Antonio and the king repented the cruel actions of the past. Prospero gave his consent to the marriage, reconciled with his brother, and forgave the king. Everyone returned to Naples.

The Characters

Prospero: The former Duke of Milan, who lost his dukedom to his brother's conniving. Too wrapped up in his books and studies, he neglected his governing, which Antonio gladly took up. His bookishness became useful when he began to study magic on the desert island.

Miranda: Prospero's beautiful and accomplished daughter. He saw to her education himself, so she was well tutored. She never knew any human but her father.

Antonio: Prospero's younger brother. He repented his evil deed.

The King of Naples: He helped see to Prospero's overthrow.

Ferdinand: The king's son. He didn't know about his father's vile deed.

Caliban: Half human, half beast.
Ariel: A magic spirit. (An optional character.)

The Plot

A magician, Prospero, and his daughter, Miranda, lived alone on a deserted island and were attended to by magical spirits and a misshapen being named Caliban, half man and half beast. One day Prospero commanded a spirit to raise a terrible storm to capsize a passing ship. Miranda begged him to spare the people on the ship, and he said he already had. Prospero told her he had brought people to the island so she could see other humans like herself.

Then he told her he had once been the Duke of Milan and she had been a princess. His brother, Antonio, conspired with the King of Naples to overthrow him. The subjects so loved Prospero that the king and duke were afraid to kill him, so they had set him and Miranda adrift at sea to die. A lord at court had secretly provisioned the boat with food, water, clothes, and books on magic. Prospero and Miranda had landed on the island, where they had been living for the last twelve years. Then Prospero told Miranda the ship's passengers included the king and Antonio.

The shipwrecked passengers and crew became separated; each one believing he was the lone survivor and the others dead, and the ship floated safe in the harbor. Prospero had a spirit bring the king's son, Ferdinand, to them. Ferdinand was upset because he believed his father was dead, but he forgot his troubles when he saw Miranda. He thought the lovely young lady was the goddess of the island. Miranda was equally taken with the handsome youth. Prospero saw they were falling in love, but wanted to test Ferdinand before he would allow his daughter to be further smitten. He told Miranda that Ferdinand wasn't the best example of what a man could be, but she said he was all she wanted. Then Prospero set Ferdinand to hard labor and made himself invisible so he could observe him.

Miranda came to talk to Ferdinand and, against her father's express command, told him her name. Soon enough, Ferdinand was professing his love and asking her to marry him. Convinced their love was true, Prospero appeared to the lovers and consented to their marriage.

Meanwhile, the spirit had been torturing the king and Antonio, reminding them of their evil deed until they begged forgiveness and repented. Prospero had the spirit bring the two to him. He forgave them, and then opened a door so they could see Ferdinand and Miranda playing chess. Prospero announced the impending marriage and announced it was a wise Providence that had seen fit that he should be driven from his dukedom so his daughter could inherit the crown of Naples. They celebrated the reconciliation and engagement that evening, and in the morning all returned to Naples. Before he left, Prospero freed his spirits and beast-slave and buried his books on magic, sure he would never need to use the art again.

How to Tell This Story

This version of the story is pared down to the minimum. If you like, you can add another character, Ariel. Ariel is the most fetching of the spirits Prospero commands, and you can give him a much larger role in the story. The witch Sycorax, who died shortly before Prospero arrived, had enchanted the desert island. She had imprisoned Ariel, along with a great many other spirits, in trees because they refused to obey her wicked commands. When Prospero first came to the island, he was just learning magic, but he knew enough to free Ariel from the enchantment that kept him painfully trapped in a tree. Then he commanded Ariel to serve him but promised to free him as soon as he had brought about a reconciliation with Antonio and the king. Ariel was very grateful to Prospero for releasing him from the tree, but he was also quite anxious to be free and asked for his freedom several times in the story. When he was freed, he saw Prospero and crew safely back to Naples and then went to live among the flowers.

Ariel takes care of most of the story's magic. Ariel brought on the storm and scattered the shipwrecked survivors all over the island. Ariel led Ferdinand to Miranda and Prospero with a song, sort of like a Pied Piper. He sang about the king, Ferdinand's father, lying beneath the sea, and Ferdinand followed the sound of the voice. It was Ariel who tortured Antonio and the king with visions that made them repent their evil deeds. He waited until they were tired and hungry and then set before them a feast that disappeared as soon as they sat down to eat. He then appeared to them as a harpy and reminded them how they had left Prospero and his infant daughter to die in a boat until they repented. Spend some time with Ariel and his magic if you want to add to this tale.

The Three Billy Goats Gruff

Summary

Three goat brothers desired to eat the lush grass on the mountainside, but they had to cross a bridge guarded by a wicked troll to get there. The oldest and biggest billy goat knocked the troll into the stream, and no one ever heard from him again. The goats got fat from the mountain grass.

The Characters

Three billy goat brothers: Hungry. The youngest was just a kid, but the oldest was strong, with an impressive set of horns.

A troll: Not the cute variety your child collects, but a nasty, smelly, mean troll who intended to eat the goats.

The Plot

Three billy goats with the family name Gruff wanted to climb a nearby mountainside to eat some grass so they could grow fat. To get to the mountain, they had to cross a bridge over a rushing mountain stream, and a goat-eating troll lived under the bridge.

The smallest goat went over the bridge first, and his hooves made a tiny trip-trap sound. The troll yelled out, "Who's that trip-trapping over my bridge?"

The youngest billy goat answered, "It is I, the youngest Billy Goat Gruff."

The troll replied, "I eat goats, and I'll eat you!"

"Oh, no, don't do that. Wait for my older brother. He's much larger and tastier than I am."

The troll thought that was sensible, so he waited. Soon the middle Billy Goat Gruff came across the bridge with a louder trip-trap sound. The troll again asked his question and learned that an even bigger goat would soon cross his bridge. So the greedy troll waited.

Very soon the biggest billy goat came across the bridge. His hooves made the loudest sound yet, and when the troll announced his intention to eat him, the biggest billy goat laughed and said, "You can try to eat me, but I'll bite you with my sharp teeth, kick you with my strong hooves, and knock you down with my big horns." And so when the troll came to eat him, the big billy goat roughed him up and butted him into the rushing stream. The goats grew nice and fat, and the troll never bothered them again.

How to Tell This Story

Children love to act out this tale, and it's short enough to do painlessly. Make a low bridge or just use some playground equipment. Your child can play all three goats and you the troll if there are just the two of you. The first billy goat makes just a little noise and has a tiny voice. The second billy goat makes a bit more noise, but the third is tremendously noisy, stomping his hooves and answering the troll in a loud voice. You'll probably have to be the troll.

The Three Little Pigs

Summary

Three pigs decided to be their own contractors and build their own houses. One built a house of straw, one built a house of sticks, one built a house of bricks. A wolf tried to blow down each house; he was successful with the first two houses, not successful with the third. When the wolf tried to get into the brick house through the chimney, he was thwarted by the pigs.

The Characters

Pig 1: A not-so-smart, lazy pig.
Pig 2: A somewhat smarter pig.
Pig 3: A smart pig.
The wolf: The big, bad wolf. A very hungry animal. He'll try anything to get at the pigs.

The Plot

Three young pigs, who lived with their mother in a cottage, left home to seek their fortunes. The first pig built a house of straw, which he bought from a merchant. (He was not smart enough and too lazy to build a house out of anything but easy-to-get straw.) Along came a wolf who said,

"Little pig, little pig
 Let me in! Let me in!
 Or I'll huff and I'll puff
 And I'll blow your house in!"

The pig answered:

"Not by the hair of my chinny-chin-chin!"

The wolf blew the lazy pig's house down with ease.

The lazy pig escaped to the second pig's house. The second pig had built a house of twigs. He worked harder and was a little smarter than the first pig. Along came the wolf, and the whole dialogue was repeated. It was a little harder, but the wolf blew down the house.

The two pigs escaped to the third pig's house. The wolf came finally to the third pig's house, which was built out of bricks. Now all three pigs were inside that house. Try as he did, the house couldn't be blown down. So the wolf tried to climb down through the chimney. Little by little, he told the pigs that he'd just put one paw, then another, then his tail, then his body, down the chimney. The pigs weren't worried, because they had put a boiling pot of water in the fireplace. "Yow!" yelled the wolf, and back up the chimney he went.

The pigs never saw the wolf again.

How to Tell This Story

The moral of this story is not that bricks are sturdier than straw; it's that you should think before you start doing something. The third pig succeeded because he took the time to think before acting.

In any event, your audience will no doubt be wondering what happened to the pigs' furniture and toys when their houses were blown down. "So the pig took his Pooh bear and went to his brother's house" could be the kind of information you can add to the story.

The Three Spinners

Summary

The queen locked a poor girl in three rooms with a supply of flax and a spinning wheel. She ordered the girl to spin the flax, and said that when she was finished she could marry the queen's eldest son. After three days of crying, the girl looked out the window and saw three ugly women. They agreed to help her if she would call them her aunts and invite them to her wedding. The women spun the flax and were invited to the wedding as promised. When the prince saw the women and learned they came by their deformities from spinning, he vowed his new wife would never touch a spinning wheel.

The Characters

A young girl: Lazy but true to her word.
The queen: Wanted an industrious wife for her son.
Three ugly women: One had a broad, flat foot. One had a large underlip that hung down over her chin. The third had a grotesquely enlarged thumb.
The prince: He did what his mama told him.

The Plot

A mother, annoyed by her daughter's relentless aversion to the spinning wheel, beat her until she cried. The queen, who was passing by, heard the cries and asked why the mother beat her girl. The embarrassed mother said it was because she couldn't get her daughter to leave the spinning wheel alone and that the family couldn't afford to buy her all the flax she needed.

The queen wanted to reward such industriousness. She took the lazy girl to the castle and put her in three rooms filled with flax from floor to ceiling. The queen said when the girl had spun all the flax, she could marry the crown prince. The girl cried for three days, because she couldn't begin to spin all that flax. The queen came and told her it was time to get to work, no matter how she missed her family.

The girl looked out the window and saw three women with strange deformities. They agreed to help her spin the rooms full of flax if she would invite them to the wedding and introduce them as her aunts. She agreed, and so they spun all the flax. The wedding was arranged.

When the new princess introduced the three unattractive women as her aunts, the prince asked the first how she had come by her flat, broad foot. She replied it had come from treading the spinning wheel. He asked the second how she had come by her large underlip, "By licking," she replied. The third had come by her broad thumb from twisting the thread. The prince proclaimed that the charming new princess would never again touch a spinning wheel.

How to Tell This Story

What matters with this story isn't that laziness is rewarded, it's that being true to your word is. (Perhaps the girl only hated to spin but enjoyed needlework.) If the laziness bothers you, have the women only help the girl spin the flax.

If you want to make the point on keeping promises a little more strong, have the lazy girl snub the three women by not inviting them to the wedding. Then they placed a dire curse on the girl to teach her a lesson. Make it a curse your child can relate to (she can't ride a bike) or something totally outlandish (a cucumber for a nose). Then solving it is equally pragmatic (the girl had to learn to inflate a bike tire) or imaginative (she had to paddle her canoe across a big lake full of sea serpents). When the curse was broken, the wedding party resumed, and the girl introduced the women as her aunts as she had promised.

What was so appealing about the prince? Have the lazy girl watch him from an open window for days and gradually fall in love with him. She could see that he was kind to animals or true to his promises from watching him. Make the prince fall in love with the girl too. Each evening she was in the rooms spinning, she was allowed to join the royal family for dinner and entertainment. The prince could fall in love with her good qualities.

Thumbelina

Summary

A woman wanted to have a baby, and a fairy gave her Thumbelina, who was only half a thumb size tall. She was kidnapped by an ugly toad who wanted her to marry his son. Then she was kidnapped by a beetle, then by a mole, both of whom had courtship in mind. Thumbelina befriended a swallow, who was very ill; the swallow invited Thumbelina to escape on his back. She met the king of the flower fairies, who was Thumbelina's size, and they married.

The Characters

Thumbelina's parents: They wanted a child and were given Thumbelina by a fairy.

The fairy: A minor character, unless you want her to be otherwise.

Thumbelina: A beautiful little woman (she was apparently born a woman) who was the tiniest human ever. She didn't even have time to think about happiness, because she was constantly being kidnapped.

The toad: Ugly; he wanted Thumbelina to marry his son.

The fish: They rescued Thumbelina, but sent her off to a worse fate.

The beetle: As ugly as the toad; he wanted to marry Thumbelina.

The field mouse: Made Thumbelina an unwilling guest.

The mole: Handsome and well dressed as moles go; he wanted to marry Thumbelina.

A swallow: Befriended by Thumbelina; he eventually rescued her.

The fairy king: A man-fairy who was the size of Thumbelina and whom Thumbelina married.

The Plot

A couple wished for a child. Their wish was granted by a fairy, who told them to plant barleycorn in a flowerpot. When the flower came up, Thumbelina was inside. (She was fully grown, though only as tall as half a thumb, and wearing a cotton dress.)

One night she was captured by a toad, who wanted Thumbelina to marry his son. To prevent Thumbelina from escaping, he placed her on a lily pad in the middle of the lake. Some fish heard Thumbelina's crying and gnawed away at the lily pad's stem so that Thumbelina would float away.

A beetle spied Thumbelina, thought that she was pretty, and lifted her off the lily pad. Thumbelina was frightened and cried. The beetle wanted to marry her. But when the beetle's friends saw Thumbelina, they said that she was ugly (as she was, in a beetle's eyes), and then the beetle decided he wanted to get rid of her. Thumbelina, evicted, lived in the woods for the entire summer until winter. Finally, in the dead of winter, she encountered a field mouse, who invited her into his den. He told Thumbelina that if she cooked and sang for him, then she could stay.

One day they had a visitor, a wealthy, handsome mole. The mole ridiculed the sun and the flowers and the trees because, well, he was a mole and stayed underground. The mole built a tunnel from his house to the field mouse's house. He described his home—the tunnels in the ground—and told Thumbelina not to worry about the dead swallow that was in the passage. Through a tiny hole in the ceiling of the tunnel, Thumbelina saw the swallow. "Poor bird," she thought. "It must have died from the cold." Thumbelina missed birds. She was sad.

The next morning Thumbelina went to visit the bird. It was very quiet, but she heard a faint "thump, thump" of his heart. She wrapped a blanket around the bird. The next day she brought some food. The swallow thanked Thumbelina for saving his life. Throughout the winter, Thumbelina cared for the bird, until the spring, when he was well enough to fly away. Thumbelina wished she could be with the swallow.

In the meantime, the field mouse prepared Thumbelina for her marriage to the mole. Months passed, and Thumbelina cried often, "I don't want to marry the mole." To which the field mouse replied, "Don't be a silly, or I'll bite you with my sharp teeth." Thumbelina prepared to say goodbye to the sun forever.

One day the swallow appeared. He told Thumbelina to climb on his back and he would take Thumbelina away. The swallow took Thumbelina to his home, a wonderful meadow. There Thumbelina saw a tiny man, as small as she, with wings. He was the king of the flower fairies. Remember: Every flower has a fairy, and this man was the king of them all. The fairy king asked Thumbelina for her hand in marriage, and Thumbelina said yes.

The flowers opened in joy. When the weather warmed, it became time for the swallow to fly north; Thumbelina and the swallow said goodbye to each other. But the swallow told everyone about Thumbelina, so that's how we know about her.

How to Tell This Story

Don't forget—Thumbelina had a life before the toad captured her. What did Thumbelina do all day? Why, she rowed in a walnut shell about the bowl of water that her parents had left out.

To Thumbelina, everything was so big. The leaves, the bugs, the raindrops, the snowflakes—everything was out of proportion. A strange world, but lots of fun.

And there are lots of questions that you might be asked, so get ready: What about Thumbelina's diapers? Where did she get clothes? Were there any tiny Thumbelina swings or playgrounds? If you're asked any of these questions, remember that what your child wants is a richer description of Thumbelina's world.

For as long as your children have their childhood—and if they're lucky it will be a long time—tell them to keep an eye out for Thumbelina. On any pretty spring or summer day she, and the flower fairy king, might be around.

Tom Thumb

Summary

A couple wished for a son and had one, but he was only as big as a thumb. The resourceful child left home to help his family, and had many adventures before making his way back to his parents.

The Characters

Tom Thumb: A mischievous but lucky child who was no bigger than a thumb.

The peasant and his wife: Tom's parents, who loved him dearly.

Two strange men: They plotted to kidnap Tom to make money.
Two robbers: They plotted to steal the parson's gold.
A cow: Swallowed Tom with her hay.
A wolf: Also swallowed Tom.

The Plot

A peasant couple wished for a son so much that they prayed they would be content with a child even if he was no bigger than a thumb. As if by magic, they had a healthy son who was no bigger than a thumb. Despite his size, Tom Thumb was lucky and resourceful, and used his size to his advantage.

One day Tom brought the woodcart to his father by whispering in the horse's ear, giving him directions. (Tom Thumb couldn't hold the reins, of course!) Two strange men observed the apparently self-directed horse—they were amazed. But they were even more astounded when they saw Tom. They offered to buy Tom from his father, who at first refused. Tom persuaded his father to take their money. He left with the two men, then escaped from them by jumping in a mouse hole.

Later that evening, two men plotted to rob the parson. Tom got their attention from his hiding place and offered to help them in their scheme. When they got to the parson's house, though, Tom intentionally made such a racket that he woke up the milkmaid and the parson; the robbers were forced to flee. Tom settled down to sleep in the parson's barn in the hay.

Tom woke up just as he was being swallowed by a cow. While inside the cow, he began to be crowded by all the hay, so he shouted, "Don't give me any more food!" This frightened the milkmaid and the pastor. They thought the cow was possessed by spirits. The parson had the cow slaughtered, but the stomach, with Tom inside, was thrown away.

A wolf happened by and found the cow's stomach with Tom inside. Tom spoke to the wolf and told him where he could get all the food he wanted—at Tom's own house, of course! The wolf followed Tom's directions to the peasant's house, where he ate his fill. The wolf was so full, in fact, that he could not fit out through the exit again. Tom then screamed for his mother and father, who killed the wolf, and rescued Tom.

How to Tell This Story

"Tom Thumb" is primarily an adventure story, and children seem to love imagining being as small as a thumb. Be sure to include as many details as you can about Tom's vantage point—sitting in a horse's ear, in a mousehole, in a cow's stomach. You can even include details from around the child's room—what would it be like being only as big as a thumb in your child's closet, for instance?

"Tom Thumb" offers an opportunity for serialized stories. It's easy to create new adventures for Tom, and these adventures can go on evening after evening. For example: Tom Thumb rides a mouse; Tom Thumb goes swimming in the sink; Tom Thumb rides a boat in the bathtub; Tom Thumb gets trapped in somebody's mail package and gets sent to California; Tom Thumb rescues toys that were trapped in cracks and behind beds.

Again, you can lengthen or shorten the story by including or excluding the various parts, which are mostly self-contained. This story can also be modernized by having Tom exploring a modern city. Maybe Tom finds himself in a department store or in a toy shop, for instance. Tom could foil the plans of bank robbers by jumping on the silent alarm button when inside the bank. He could get thrown out with the garbage and swallowed by a garbage truck instead of a cow, and return home inside a recycling bin.

The Twelve Brothers

Summary

The king, father of twelve boys, told the queen that if the next child was a girl, he would kill the boys. The queen couldn't bear the thought of losing her boys, and so she hid them in the forest so they could grow up. The princess grew up thinking she was an only child but one day discovered she had twelve brothers. The princess set out to find her brothers. She found them and moved into their cottage. One day she cut down twelve lilies in the garden, and her innocent action turned her brothers into ravens. A witch told her she must remain silent for seven years for the ravens to become men again, so the princess grabbed a spinning wheel and climbed a tree to wait out her seven years. In time, a king came along, and they were married. Her mother-in-law hated her, and toward the end of the seven years convinced the king that he needed to burn the princess at the stake because she wouldn't talk. As the flames were licking her feet, the seven years came to an end, and twelve ravens that had been circling the fire turned into her brothers, who rushed forward to save the princess. Then she could explain everything to the king, who forgave her—and she, him. They all lived happily ever after, except the mother-in-law, who was miserable.

The Characters

Twelve brothers: The youngest, Benjamin, was most significant. After they had to hide in the forest to stay alive, they hated girls.

The princess: She was very good and cleaned and cooked for her brothers in their cottage even though she was royalty. Kind and gentle. Beautiful, of course. She had a golden star on her forehead.

The king: Listened to his mother too much.
The queen mother: Mean.

The Plot

The king, who had already fathered twelve boys, wanted a baby girl, so he told the pregnant queen that if their next child was a girl, he would kill the boys. He ordered twelve little coffins to be made. The queen couldn't keep this secret and so showed the youngest boy, Benjamin, the coffins. She told him he and his brothers should go hide in the woods and climb the highest tree daily to watch for a signal flag from the tower castle. A white flag would mean the baby was a boy, and it was safe to return. A red flag meant a girl. The boys hid in the woods, and on the twelfth day when, Benjamin climbed the highest tree, he saw a red flag.

The boys, justifiably angry, swore to kill any maiden they found, and then they made their home in an enchanted cottage deep in the forest. Benjamin cleaned and cooked, because he was the youngest, and his brothers hunted each day.

Ten years passed, and back at the castle on wash day, the young princess noticed twelve shirts in the laundry. When she asked about them, the queen had to tell her kind and beautiful daughter about her brothers, and she showed the girl the twelve little coffins. And so the princess took the twelve shirts and ventured out to find her brothers. In time a lovely young woman with a golden star on her forehead knocked on the cottage door when Benjamin was there alone, and because he was impressed with her royal bearing and beauty, he let her in instead of killing her. The princess told him she was looking for her twelve lost brothers and showed him the shirts. They were very happy to have found one another, but Benjamin warned her his brothers would kill her if they found her, so she must hide.

When the brothers returned, Benjamin made them promise not to kill the first maiden they found, and then he revealed their sister. They too were impressed with her delicate beauty and royal bearing and loved her immediately. She stayed with them in the cottage and helped Benjamin during the day while the older boys hunted. Everyone was wonderfully cozy and content.

One day, she prepared a great feast for the brothers, and after they ate, thought to please them with twelve lilies she picked from the garden. But when she picked the flowers, the brothers turned into ravens and flew away. The house and garden disappeared, and the princess was alone in the woods. An old woman who was standing in the woods told the princess that the only way to release her brothers from the spell that made them ravens was to remain silent for seven years, not speaking or singing or laughing. And if she made a peep during that time, her brothers would die. That seemed reasonable to the princess, so she climbed a tree and set about spinning to pass the time.

Soon enough a king hunting in the woods noticed the lovely princess with the golden star on her forehead and asked her to become his wife. She nodded her assent and came down from the tree. They were married, but the young queen never spoke or laughed even though over six years had passed.

Now, the queen mother had never liked the queen, and she told the king that his mute wife was probably a beggar. Worst yet, she never laughed. In time, the queen mother persuaded the king to burn the queen at the stake. Still the queen remained silent.

Just as the flames were about to consume the queen, the seven years came to an end and twelve ravens swooped from the sky to save the queen, changing into the twelve brothers. She was able to explain everything to the king, and they were reconciled and everyone lived out their lives in happiness—except for the queen mother, who died miserably.

How to Tell This Story

If you're expecting, this is not the story to tell your child. Try softening the edges a bit by having the king merely banish the brothers to live in the enchanted forest. Better yet, have one of the boys hear the king mutter to himself how he'd trade his boys for one little girl, so they all run away to live in the enchanted woods. Make the king, queen, and princess mourn for the return of the boys. The king and queen realize that while girls are very special, so are boys. They miss the rambunctious lot of them. Make up stories about the individual charms they miss about each boy, ways that illustrate your own child's endearing qualities. If your child wears yellow rain boots on sunny days, have one of the princes do the same. Your child loves to recognize parts of himself in stories, so it's always fun to include these sidelines.

Instead of marrying off the princess, reconcile the whole family. When the princess finds the boys, she can bring them back to the castle so the king will apologize and give each of the young princes his own dog.

If you remain true to the story, spend some time describing how the princess communicated when she had to be silent. How did she tell her servants what she wanted to eat? Have your child try to be silent for some time while you go about your daily routine.

The Twelve Dancing Princesses

Summary

The king suspected the twelve royal sisters were sneaking away every night for a little gaiety, because each morning their slippers were worn and torn, danced to pieces. Presum-

ably they were sleeping late too. When he couldn't find a way
to control them, the king offered any man in the kingdom his
choice of the girls in marriage as well as his kingdom in return
for solving the mystery. Many princes tried and failed, and so
they lost their lives. But a down-on-his luck soldier met up
with a mysterious crone who told him how to find out where
the girls went. He succeeded where others failed and so took
the eldest girl in marriage and inherited the kingdom upon the
king's death.

The Characters

The soldier: The lucky underdog who got to marry a princess
   and inherit a kingdom.
The king: He couldn't figure out what his girls were doing all
   night, every night.
Twelve princesses: They liked the nightlife. Most significant
   are the eldest and the youngest.

The Plot

These twelve princesses, each more beautiful than the
other, slept in closely placed beds in a large hall. Even though
the door to their room was locked and bolted, each morning
the sisters' shoes appeared under their beds worn and torn.
How did the girls wear their shoes out each night? The king
surmised the girls were dancing their shoes to bits and put out
a general announcement to the kingdom. Any man who could
find out where the sisters went each night could have his
choice of them in marriage, and he would inherit the throne.
The king gave them three nights to find out.

Of course, many princes rose to the challenge, but each lost
his life in the quest. Those who came forward were treated royally and given a room adjacent to the princesses' room so they
could watch them through the night. But not a one of them was
able to stay awake through the night, so they all were beheaded.

Along came a young soldier, recently discharged from the army because his wounds made him unable to serve. He had no plans or any real future, but as luck would have it, along the road he met an old woman. He joked to her that he would like to solve the mystery, marry a princess, and inherit the kingdom. To his surprise, the woman took him seriously and gave him some good advice: "Don't drink the wine at the castle, because it's drugged." Then she gave him a magical cloak that made him invisible.

The soldier went to the castle to accept the challenge. Like the others before him, he was treated well and dressed in royal clothes. But when a princess brought a glass of wine to his room before bed, he only pretended to drink it and let the wine run down to a sponge he had concealed under his chin. He then feigned sleep.

Because the door between his room and the sisters' was open, he could see everything they did. As soon as they thought he was asleep, they began to dress in their finery and primp before mirrors. The youngest sister sensed something was up, though, and told her sisters she thought something unfortunate was about to happen. The oldest ridiculed her and told her they had nothing to worry about—the soldier was unlikely to succeed where princes had failed.

When they were all perfectly coiffed and fashionably dressed, a sister knocked on one of the beds, which descended to reveal a secret passage. The sisters descended, with the eldest leading and the youngest taking up the rear. Quick as a wink, the soldier donned his cloak that made him invisible and followed. On the way, he stepped on the hem of the youngest sister's dress. She cried out, but the eldest sister told her to be quiet and said that her dress was probably caught on a nail.

They traveled quite a way underground and soon reached a magical place where the trees had leaves of silver, gold, and diamonds. The soldier couldn't control himself and reached out to take samples of each. When the twigs snapped, the youngest sister again was scared, but the eldest quieted her and mocked the very idea of the soldier being able to discover their secret. The princesses were met by twelve princes, who each took one of the girls and rowed her across a lake to a brightly lit castle where music played. The soldier hitched a ride on the boat with the youngest princess and her prince.

At the castle, the princesses swirled and twirled, dancing the night away. The soldier danced invisibly and enjoyed himself marvelously. When the dancers paused for refreshment, the soldier would drain the wine from the princesses' cups before they could drink any themselves. This made the youngest afraid, but her eldest sister again silenced her.

As morning neared, the princesses rode back across the lake with their princes, and the soldier hitched a ride with the eldest this time. He ran ahead quickly, jumped into bed, and pretended to be asleep as the princesses returned to their room. As they undressed and put their worn-out shoes beneath their beds, they again scorned the efforts of the soldier.

The soldier decided not to tell anyone what he had seen, but returned for two more nights, because he had a great time at the party. On the third night, he took a wine cup as a souvenir. So when the king summoned the soldier to learn what he had discovered, he took his precious leaves and the wine cup as evidence. He told the king the sisters went each night to an underground castle to dance with princes. When the king asked the princesses if it was true, they confessed.

The soldier picked the eldest sister as his wife, because she was close to his age, and they were married that very day.

How to Tell This Story

If you find some aspects of this story unpalatable, it's easy enough to change some details without eliminating the delightful magic cloak and underground castle. You can say the princesses were enchanted by the evil princes and forced to dance each night, and then the soldier became a savior, not a snitch. This also keeps the sisters from being willfully disobedient. Instead of being forced to quit visiting the underground castle, maybe the princesses could discover on their own the dangers of disobeying their father. Maybe the princes tried to turn them into swans on the lake or silver leaves on the tree, and the soldier and the king saved them. The youngest sister's fears of discovery provide a good chance to talk about misbehavior. She was the only one who felt they would be discovered, and she didn't listen to her inner voice.

You might not like to tell a story in which a young woman is offered as a reward like so much gold. Make the reward a chest of jewels or a bicycle, whatever might appeal to your child. Maybe the ending bothers you. The soldier doesn't necessarily have to marry anyone in the story; he could go away on an adventure with his magic cloak. What else might he do with a cloak that rendered him invisible? (What would your child do with one?) Maybe all the underground princes could come aboveground for a party. Or you could make the soldier and sister fall in love during the story instead of being thrust together at the end. (A French version of this tale has the youngest sister fall in love with a young gardener who discovers the girls' secret.) Perhaps the princess of choice shared an interest in archery with the soldier and they fell in love during the banquets on the three nights. Maybe something happened on the boats.

This tale becomes lots of fun if you start designing small subplots about the sisters and the princes. You can introduce a different one each time. Have the second prince's pet dragon come to one of the parties, describe the underground kingdom in great detail, draw out the history of the soldier—perhaps he was unfairly treated in the army. You might even create a prince or princess surprisingly like your child.

The Ugly Duckling

Summary

An ugly duck was ridiculed and picked on by the whole duckyard because of his looks, so he ran away, meeting several other birds and animals, who likewise show him cruelty and misunderstanding. He finally found out that he wasn't a duck at all, but a fledgling swan!

The Characters

The ugly duckling: An ugly, lonely duck. (But not really.)

The sitting duck: The ugly duck's mother, who tried to defend the duck.

The duckyard ducks: The ugly duckling's siblings and neighbors, who made fun of the ugly duckling and picked on him.

The wild ducks: They lived in a great marsh.

The hunting dogs: They picked up the wild ducks that had been shot.

The cat and the hen: Named Sonnie and Chickie-Low-Legs respectively, these self-centered pets tried to educate the ugly duckling to purr and cluck and to be just like them.

The peasant family: A simple family who rescued the duckling from a frozen lake.

The swans: The ugly duckling's final companions.

The Plot

An ugly duckling was born to a duck family. The mother believed he was so ungainly because he had been in the egg too long. The mother knew that the ugly duckling was good, but despite her efforts, the rest of the ducks and hens all picked on the duck because of his unusual looks. The duckling finally ran away.

He reached a marsh of wild ducks, who teased him. But then hunters killed some of the ducks. The rest of the wild ducks tried to fly away, but many more were shot dead by the hunter's gun. One hunting dog approached the ugly duckling, but the dog left the ugly duckling alone because he was so ugly.

Because all of the duck's companions were either dead or had flown away, the ugly duckling moved on. He came upon an old woman's cabin, where he met a cat and hen. The cat and the hen were self-centered animals, always referring to "we and the rest of the world." They tried to teach the duckling to be just like them. The duckling felt drawn to the water, though, and left the cat and hen.

The duckling found a lake to float on, but when winter arrived, he froze to the ice. A peasant rescued him, but the ugly duckling thought that the peasant wanted to cook and eat him, so he escaped.

After a cold, rough winter, spring returned. The duckling, feeling all alone and miserable, approached a group of swans. To his surprise, they welcomed him. He looked at his reflection in the water and found that during the long, hard winter he had turned into a beautiful swan. He was finally happy.

How to Tell This Story

"The Ugly Duckling" is the perfect tale to tell your children if they feel different from other children. But they certainly don't have to feel ugly. The story can be changed only slightly to make the duckling unique or unusual instead of ugly; you can show him to be born with special traits or talents that simply aren't yet appreciated by his small-minded fellows. Emphasize the point that it took a while for the duckling to find his own gang, but eventually he did.

Have the other ducklings see the ugly duckling when he

was full-grown and realize that he was actually very beautiful. (They're willing to admit a mistake.)

What does a swan look like? Many children are familiar with ducks. (The most exciting day in my daughter's life was when, at about eighteen months, she went to "feed duckies" in West Virginia.) But a swan? Spend some time comparing the two fowl; kids want to know.

Children will enjoy this story if you make use of the sounds and noises in it. The ducks quack-quack, the hens cluck-cluck, the cat purrs, the dogs pant and splash, and the swans honk. Pretty soon your children will be making all the sounds with you.

The Valiant Little Tailor

Summary

A tailor, who was a little cheap, and a little hasty but very clever, got caught in circumstances that put his cleverness and bravado to the test. He killed seven flies at once, and inscribed the message "Seven with one blow" on his belt buckle. This message served to intimidate a giant into believing the tailor was a great warrior. Through a series of other tricks, the tailor got the giant to believe that he could do all sorts of things, and thus the tailor prevented himself from being eaten. A king heard of the tailor's exploits and wanted the tailor to marry his daughter. The king put the tailor through a series of tests, and even tried to have him killed once he heard that the tailor really was just a tailor. In the end, the king, too, was convinced that the tailor was strong, brave, invincible. Eventually the tailor became king.

The Characters

The tailor: Substance or mere puffery? Fortunately, this is just a fairy tale to tell, and not the subject of a term paper. The tailor, it appears, learned the power of form over substance, and became bolder and bolder at using cleverness to thwart his opponents. The tailor was smart—at least smarter than most. But he was not all that interested in others' welfare.

The old woman: A needy person.

The giant: Big, but not brainy.

Two other giants: Also able to be deceived by the tailor.

The king: Tried to be a good king, but he was overwhelmed by the tailor's prowess.

The princess: She knew that the tailor was really just a tailor, but since nobody would accept that, there was nothing she could do about it.

The Plot

The tailor bought four ounces of jam from an old woman. (Why couldn't he have bought more? she wondered.) The jam quickly attracted seven flies, which the tailor killed with a single blow with his belt. The tailor was amazed at his own skill and bravery and inscribed in his belt buckle: "Seven at one blow." He felt exhilarated and brave and set out on a journey with some old cheese in one pocket, and a bird he found in another pocket.

On his journey he saw a giant, who threatened to kill him. The tailor told the giant to read his belt, and the giant was concerned. But the giant wanted proof, and challenged the tailor to a rock-tossing contest. The tailor won, because he said that he could toss a rock so high that it would never come back to earth—he threw the bird up.

The giant squeezed a rock and water came out. "Can you beat that?" he demanded. The tailor proved that he could get milk from stone by squeezing the cheese until whey came out.

Indeed, the giant was amazed at the tailor's strength, but he hoped he could win at some other skill. The giant said, "So you can throw and squeeze, but can you carry? Help me carry a tree out of the forest."

The tailor agreed. "You carry the trunk, and I'll carry the leaves and branches—after all, they're the largest part." Finally the giant had to stop, because the tree was too heavy. When the giant let go, the tailor was flung into the air by the branch he had been holding. "Ah ha," said the giant. "You can't even hold on to a branch."

The tailor replied that he had jumped over the tree because he thought he heard hunters coming. "You jump over the tree," the tailor said. But the giant just got caught in the branches.

The giant told the tailor that he was valiant, and offered the tailor a place in his cave and all the fruit and meat the tailor could eat. After dinner, the tailor went to sleep, but found that the spot the giant offered was uncomfortable. So the tailor moved to another spot, using his coat as a pillow.

When the giant thought that the tailor was asleep, he decided to kill the tailor. So he took a large stick and hit what he thought was the tailor's head—only the tailor had moved! In the morning the giant was amazed to see the tailor, and thought he had come back to life. He fled from the tailor.

The tailor wandered until he came to the king's palace, where he offered to be of service. When the king's soldiers saw the tailor's belt, they refused to fight alongside him. The king wanted to get rid of the tailor, but was afraid. So the king sent the tailor on a mission: Kill two giants that lived nearby, and win the hand of the king's daughter along with half the kingdom.

The tailor found the giants sleeping by a stream. Stealthily, he threw rocks at one giant's head. The giant accused his companion of throwing rocks at him. After arguing for a while, they went back to sleep. The tailor then threw a heavy rock at the other giant. Now the two giants argued about rock throwing and calling each other a liar; they then got into a fight and finally killed each other. In the process, they uprooted trees. When the tailor reported his victory to the king, he said, "The giants tried to kill me with these trees."

But the king wasn't ready to give the tailor his daughter and half the kingdom. So the king told the tailor to capture the fierce unicorn that lived in the forest. When the tailor found the unicorn, the unicorn charged the tailor, but got his horn caught in a tree. At that point, it was no trouble roping the creature and bringing him to the king.

Still, the king insisted on one more test: capturing a wild boar that had been tearing up the meadowland. The boar chased the tailor into a nearby church. The tailor bolted in, and then jumped out the window. When the boar entered the church, the tailor shut the door and captured the boar.

Finally, the king had to keep his promise. There was a wedding—held without much ceremony—and the tailor became a king. But on their wedding night, the princess, now a queen, heard the tailor talking in his sleep: "Stitch left, more thread here, tighten those buttons," she heard.

The queen told her father that the tailor was not a hero, but just a tailor. She wanted to be rid of the tailor. Her father told her to leave her bedroom door open, and while the tailor slept, he would be captured, then exiled. But one of the king's servants told the tailor about the plot. So that night the tailor pretended to talk in his sleep: "Sew quickly, or I shall have to kill you. Sew well, or I shall kill your family, too. For I have slain giants, captured a unicorn, and hunted a wild boar. I'm not afraid of anybody standing outside my bedroom door."

When the servants heard this, they ran away in fear. The tailor remained king.

How to Tell This Story

There are plenty of messages here, if you decide that you want to talk about morals. The question of form versus substance is the largest issue. But another is: Don't believe everything you read, such as a tailor's belt. If you're inclined to teach your children that not everything an adult utters is true, this is a good place to start.

Between each adventure and the king's *not* keeping his promise, you can add a refrain: "Was the king going to keep his promise? No, not yet." Repetition is always fun for children.

The marriage between the princess and tailor seems to lack depth. It might be better if she makes a deal with the tailor. He continues to make fine clothes for her *and* for the poor people of the kingdom, and she won't reveal who he is. In many ways, this is a more satisfying ending.

The White Hare and the Crocodiles

Summary

A white hare who lived on an island tricked the river crocodiles into helping him cross to the mainland. Then he made them so angry by taunting them that they pulled out all of his hair and left him naked and cold. A passing group of boys played a trick on the hare that made him even more uncomfortable. A kind man then helped the hare get his fur back.

The Characters

A white hare: He was smart but couldn't keep it to himself. He lived on the island of Oki, across the sea from Inaba, a province on the Japanese mainland.

The crocodiles: Lots of them lived in the sea, enough to form a bridge to the mainland. They couldn't stand to be taunted and were very quick-tempered. They also ran faster than the hare anticipated.

The rude boys: They were cruel, and were on their way to Inaba to ask Princess Yakami there to marry one of them.

Okuni: The kind boy. He was the half brother of the rude boys and the great-great-great-grandson of the younger brother of the Sun Goddess.

Yakami: The princess.

The Plot

A white hare living on Oki desperately wanted to go to the mainland, but there was no way for him to get there. So each day he would sit and gaze at the distant land and sigh. One day he noticed a crocodile swimming in the sea and thought the reptile would carry him to the mainland, but then he decided it would be safer to trick the crocodile into carrying him. So he struck up a conversation with the crocodile.

The crocodile was a bit lonely and happy to chat. They played some games together, and then the hare wondered to the crocodile if there weren't more hares on the island than crocodiles in the sea. The hare challenged him to call together enough crocodiles to stretch from the island to the mainland so he could count them all. The crocodile called all of his brethren together, and the hare hopped from crocodile back to crocodile back, counting aloud. When the hare got to the mainland, though, he didn't thank the crocodiles but jeered at them for cooperating with his plan. Immediately they became angry, chased the hare, and caught him. They pulled out his fur, a tuft at a time, saying, "This serves you right." They left the hare naked and shivering on the beach.

Before long, a group of well-dressed boys came along, and they heard the hare crying. The hare lifted his head from between his paws and told them his story. One of the boys told the hare to bathe in the salty seawater and then sit in the wind to make his fur grow back again. Of course, the procedure only made the little hare even more uncomfortable, because it pulled his skin taut and made it stiff. He cried all the harder and rolled in the sand in agony.

A lone boy carrying a great load passed next, but when he asked what was wrong, the hare ignored him and continued to cry, because he had learned not to trust people. But the boy, Okuni, spoke to the hare kindly, and eventually the hare answered with his story. When Okuni had heard the tale, he reprimanded the hare and told him his own deceit had brought his discomfort about, but he knew how to help him. The boy told the hare to go wash well in the fresh pond water and then to pick some cattails, place them on the ground, and roll in them. Then the hare's fur would return as lush as before. The hare did as he was told, his pain stopped, and his fur grew back. The hare knelt at Okuni's feet to give thanks and asked who the boy was.

Okuni told him he was the half brother of the boys who had tricked him. He said he was following them with their gear on their journey to visit Princess Yakami, whom they intended to ask to marry one of them. The hare predicted the princess would refuse to marry any of the cruel brothers and would prefer Okuni because he had such a good heart.

And the hare was right. When Yakami saw Okuni, the great-great-great-grandson of the younger brother of the Sun Goddess, she went to him and they were married.

How to Tell This Story

Count out all the crocodiles as high as your child can count at the beginning of the story. Say, "There were twenty crocodiles in the river, and the hare counted them as he crossed on their backs. One, two . . ." Have your child count aloud with you.

If you want, you can add to the hare's misery by dragging out the torture. Have the bad brothers come by singly and tell the hare to rub sand on his dry skin, roll in nettles, or anger

some bees into stinging him. Then when Okuni appears, the
hare must be won over by his goodness.

The Wind and the Sun

Summary

The Wind and Sun had an argument over who was stronger.
They decided to slug it out. In the end, the Sun won.

The Characters

The Sun: Warm, friendly, and gentle.
The Wind: Cold, forceful. The Wind started the argument.
The man: The victim. Who will get him to remove his coat?
Read on.

The Plot

The Wind started an argument with the Sun over who was
stronger. "I am the stronger," they each said. After several
days of arguing, they agreed to a competition.

The Sun said that whoever got the man walking down the
street to remove his coat would be the stronger. The Wind
said it would win.

So the Wind blew and blew. As colder and colder air surrounded the man, he drew his coat more tightly around his
neck. Finally the Wind grew tired and gave up.

Then it was the Sun's turn. As the sun smiled, the air got
warmer. The man loosened his coat, then removed it alto-
gether.

What the Wind could not achieve through force, the Sun
accomplished with gentleness.

How to Tell This Story

There are several stories within this one. It's not important to hammer in the moral—eventually your child will understand the lesson. The most interesting aspect of this story is the difference between the cool Wind and warm Sun. They make us do different things, and it's these things that are fascinating to a child.

A Wolf and Little Daughter

Summary

A little girl was picking flowers outside her garden, far from the protection of a fence. A wolf came along and threatened to eat her unless she stood still and sang a song. Slowly she slunk toward the safety of the fence.

The Characters

Little Daughter: A girl, somewhere between the ages of eight and twelve. She clearly knows about animals.
The wolf: Hungry, but not an ordinary wolf. He's a mythical creature.

The Plot

Once upon a time, Little Daughter was picking flowers outside the fenced-in yard. She did this even though her father had told her never to go outside the gate, and even though she had told her father she never would.

While she was outside, a wolf came by. The wolf told Little Daughter to sing a pretty, soft song.

Little Daughter sang, *Tray-bla, tray-bla, cum qua, kimo,**
and the wolf looked away.

Little Daughter tiptoed toward the gate, but her tiptoeing
made noise—*pitter-pat, pitter-pat, pitter-pat*—and the wolf
heard her. "I think you moved," said the wolf.

"Oh no," said Little Daughter. "I wouldn't do that, because
you told me not to."

"Sing me a pretty, soft song," the wolf said. And Little
Daughter sang the same song again.

Bit by bit, Little Daughter got closer to the gate, though
she had to sing the song each time. The singing and pitter-
patting happened several times until Little Daughter reached
the gate. She was safe.

How to Tell This Story

This African-American tale has a strong, dreamlike style
to it. It's completely fanciful, and a little unbelievable. It's a
quick tale that expresses a relationship: Both the wolf and little girl really just wanted to do what nature had designed
them to do. The story is almost a song itself; don't neglect its
musical qualities when you tell it: Repeat the melody of the
song and the *pitter-pat* again and again. This story is almost a
lullaby.

*From *The People Could Fly: American Black Folktales*, told by
Virginia Hamilton (New York: Knopf, 1985), p. 61.